THE GOLD HUNTERS

A Story of Life and Adventure in the Hudson Bay Wilds

BY JAMES OLIVER CURWOOD

909

To the sweet-voiced, dark-eyed little half-Cree maiden at Lac-Bain, who is the Minnetaki of this story; and to "Teddy" Brown, guide and trapper, and loyal comrade of the author in many of his adventures, this book is affectionately dedicated.

Contents

CHAPTER I

THE PURSUIT OF THE HUDSON BAY MAIL

The deep hush of noon hovered over the vast solitude of Canadian forest. The moose and caribou had fed since early dawn, and were resting quietly in the warmth of the February sun; the lynx was curled away in his niche between the great rocks, waiting for the sun to sink farther into the north and west before resuming his marauding adventures; the fox was taking his midday slumber and the restless moose-birds were fluffing themselves lazily in the warm glow that was beginning to melt the snows of late winter.

It was that hour when the old hunter on the trail takes off his pack, silently gathers wood for a fire, eats his dinner and smokes his pipe, eyes and ears alert;—that hour when if you speak above a whisper, he will say to you,

"Sh-h-h-h! Be quiet! You can't tell how near we are to game. Everything has had its morning feed and is lying low. The game won't be moving again for an hour or two, and there may be moose or caribou a gunshot ahead. We couldn't hear them—now!"

And yet, after a time one thing detached itself from this lifeless solitude. At first it was nothing more than a spot on the sunny side of a snow-covered ridge. Then it moved, stretched itself like a dog, with its forefeet extended far to the front and its shoulders hunched low—and was a wolf.

A wolf is a heavy sleeper after a feast. A hunter would have said that this wolf had gorged itself the night before. Still, something had alarmed it. Faintly there came to this wilderness outlaw that most thrilling of all things to the denizens of the forest—the scent of man. He came down the ridge with the slow indifference of a full-fed animal, and with only a half of his old cunning; trotted across the softening snow of an opening and stopped where the man-scent was so strong that he lifted his head straight up to the sky and sent out to his comrades in forest and plain the warning signal that he had struck a human trail. A wolf will do this, and no more, in broad day. At night he might follow, and others would join him in the chase; but with daylight about him he gives the warning and after a little slinks away from the trail.

But something held this wolf. There was a mystery in the air which puzzled him. Straight ahead there ran the broad, smooth trail of a sled and the footprints of many dogs. Sometime within the last hour the "dog mail" from Wabinosh House had passed that way on its long trip to civilization. But it was not the swift passage of man and dog that held the wolf rigidly alert, ready for flight—and yet hesitating. It was something from the opposite direction, from the North, out of which the wind was coming. First it was sound; then it was scent—then both, and the wolf sped in swift flight up the sunlit ridge.

In the direction from which the alarm came there stretched a small lake, and on its farther edge, a quarter of a mile away, there suddenly darted out from the dense rim of balsam forest a jumble of dogs and sledge and man. For a few moments the mass of animals seemed entangled in some kind of wreck or engaged in one of those fierce battles in which the half-wild sledge-dogs of the North frequently engage, even on the trail. Then there came the sharp, commanding cries of a human voice, the cracking of a whip, the yelping of the huskies, and the disordered team straightened itself and came like a yellowish-gray streak across the smooth surface of the lake. Close beside the sledge ran the man. He was tall, and thin, and even at that distance one would have recognized him as an Indian. Hardly had the team and its wild-looking driver progressed a quarter of the distance across the lake when there came a shout farther back, and a second sledge burst into view from out of the thick forest. Beside this sledge, too, a driver was running with desperate speed.

The leader now leaped upon his sledge, his voice rising in sharp cries of exhortation, his whip whirling and cracking over the backs of his dogs. The second driver still ran, and thus gained upon the team ahead, so that when they came to the opposite side of the lake, where the wolf had sent out the warning cry to his people, the twelve dogs of the two teams were almost abreast.

Quickly there came a slackening in the pace set by the leading dog of each team, and half a minute later the sledges stopped. The dogs flung themselves down in their harness, panting, with gaping jaws, the snow reddening under their bleeding feet. The men, too, showed signs of terrible strain. The elder of these, as we have said, was an Indian, pure breed of the great Northern wilderness. His companion was a youth who had not yet reached his twenties, slender, but with the strength and agility of an animal in his limbs, his handsome face bronzed by the free life of the forest, and in his veins a plentiful strain of that blood which made his comrade kin.

In those two we have again met our old friends Mukoki and Wabigoon: Mukoki, the faithful old warrior and pathfinder, and Wabigoon, the adventurous half-Indian son of the factor of Wabinosh House. Both were at the height of some great excitement. For a few moments, while gaining breath, they gazed silently into each other's face.

"I'm afraid—we can't—catch them, Muky," panted the younger. "What do you think—"

He stopped, for Mukoki had thrown himself on his knees in the snow a dozen feet in front of the teams. From that point there ran straight ahead of them the trail of the dog mail. For perhaps a full minute he examined the imprints of the dogs' feet and the smooth path made by the sledge. Then he looked up, and with one of those inimitable chuckles which meant so much when coming from him, he said:

"We catch heem—sure! See—sledge heem go *deep*. Both ride. Big load for dogs. We catch heem—sure!"

"But our dogs!" persisted Wabigoon, his face still filled with doubt. "They're completely bushed, and my leader has gone lame. See how they're bleeding!"

The huskies, as the big wolfish sledge-dogs of the far North are called, were indeed in a pitiable condition. The warm sun had weakened the hard crust of the snow until at every leap the feet of the animals had broken through, tearing and wounding themselves on its ragged, knife-like edges. Mukoki's face became more serious as he carefully examined the teams.

"Bad—ver' bad," he grunted. "We fool—fool!"

"For not bringing dog shoes?" said Wabigoon. "I've got a dozen shoes on my sledge—enough for three dogs. By George—" He leaped quickly to his toboggan, caught up the dog moccasins, and turned again to the old Indian, alive with new excitement. "We've got just one chance, Muky!" he half shouted.

"Pick out the strongest dogs. One of us must go on alone!"

The sharp commands of the two adventurers and the cracking of Mukoki's whip brought the tired and bleeding animals to their feet. Over the pads of three of the largest and strongest were drawn the buckskin moccasins, and to these three, hitched to Wabigoon's sledge, were added six others that appeared to have a little endurance still left in them. A few moments later the long line of dogs was speeding swiftly over the trail of the Hudson Bay mail, and beside the sled ran Wabigoon.

Thus this thrilling pursuit of the dog mail had continued since early dawn. For never more than a minute or two at a time had there been a rest. Over mountain and lake, through dense forest and across barren plain man and dog had sped without food or drink, snatching up mouthfuls of snow here and there—always their eyes upon the fresh trail of the flying mail. Even the fierce huskies seemed to understand that the chase had become a matter of life and death, and that they were to follow the trail ahead of them, ceaselessly and without deviation, until the end of their masters was accomplished. The human scent was becoming stronger and stronger in their wolf-like nostrils. Somewhere on that trail there were men, and other dogs, and they were to overtake them!

Even now, bleeding and stumbling as they ran, the blood of battle, the excitement of the chase, was hot within them. Half-wolf, half-dog, their white fangs snarling as stronger whiffs of the man-smell came to them, they were filled with the savage desperation of the youth who urged them on. The keen instinct of the wild pointed out their road to them, and they needed no guiding hand. Faithful until the last they dragged on their burden, their tongues lolling farther from their jaws, their hearts growing weaker, their eyes bloodshot until they glowed like red balls. Now and then, when he had run until his endurance was gone, Wabigoon would fling himself upon the sledge to regain breath and rest his limbs, and the dogs would tug harder, scarce slackening their speed under the increased weight. Once a huge moose crashed through the forest a hundred paces away, but the huskies paid no attention to it; a little farther on a lynx, aroused from his sun bath on a rock, rolled like a great gray ball across the trail,—the dogs cringed but for an instant at the sight of this mortal enemy of theirs, and then went on.

Slower and slower grew the pace. The rearmost dog was now no more than a drag, and reaching a keen-edged knife far out over the end of the sledge Wabi severed his breast strap and the exhausted animal rolled out free beside the trail. Two others of the team were pulling scarce a pound, another was running lame, and the trail behind was spotted with pads of blood. Each minute added to the despair that was growing in the youth's face. His eyes, like those of his faithful dogs, were red from the terrible strain of the race, his lips were parted, his legs, as tireless as those of a red deer, were weakening under him. More and more frequently he flung himself upon the sledge, panting for breath, and shorter and shorter became his intervals of running between these periods of rest. The end of the chase was almost at hand. They could not overtake the Hudson Bay mail!

With a final cry of encouragement Wabi sprang from the sledge and plunged along at the head of the dogs, urging them on in one last supreme effort. Ahead of them was a break in the forest trail and beyond that, mile upon mile, stretched the vast white surface of Lake Nipigon. And far out in the glare of sun and snow there moved an object, something that was no more than a thin black streak to Wabi's blinded eyes but which he knew was the dog mail on its way to civilization. He tried to shout, but the sound that fell from his lips could not have been heard a hundred paces away; his limbs tottered beneath him; his feet seemed suddenly to turn into lead, and he sank helpless into the snow. The faithful pack crowded about him licking his face and hands, their hot breath escaping between their gaping jaws like hissing steam For a few moments it seemed to the Indian youth that day had suddenly turned into night. His eyes closed, the panting of the dogs came to him more and more faintly, as if they were moving away; he felt himself sinking, sinking slowly down into utter blackness.

Desperately he fought to bring himself back into life. There was one more chance—just one! He heard the dogs again, he felt their tongues upon his hands and face, and he dragged himself to his knees, groping out with his hands like one who had gone blind. A few feet away was the sledge, and out there, far beyond his vision now, was the Hudson Bay mail!

Foot by foot he drew himself out from among the tangle of dogs. He reached the sledge, and his fingers gripped convulsively at the cold steel of his rifle. One more chance! One more chance! The words—the thought—filled his brain, and he raised the rifle to his shoulder, pointing its muzzle up to the sky so that he would not harm the dogs. And then, once, twice, five times he fired into the air, and at the end of the fifth shot he drew fresh cartridges from his belt, and fired again and again, until the black streak far out in the wilderness of ice and snow stopped in its progress—and turned back. And still the sharp signals rang out again and again, until the barrel of Wabi's rifle grew hot, and his cartridge belt was empty.

Slowly the gloom cleared away before his eyes. He heard a shout, and staggered to his feet, stretching out his arms and calling a name as the dog mail stopped half a hundred yards from his own team.

With something between a yell of joy and a cry of astonishment a youth of about Wabi's age sprang from the second sleigh and ran to the Indian boy, catching him in his arms as for a second time, he sank fainting upon the snow.

"Wabi—what's the matter?" he cried. "Are you hurt? Are you—"

For a moment Wabigoon struggled to overcome his weakness.

"Rod—" he whispered, "Rod—Minnetaki—"

His lips ceased to move and he sank heavily in his companion's arms.

"What is it, Wabi? Quick! Speak!" urged the other. His face had grown strangely white, his voice trembled. "What about—Minnetaki?"

Again the Indian youth fought to bring himself back to life. His words came faintly,

"Minnetaki—has been captured—by—the—Woongas!"

Then even his breath seemed to stop, and he lay like one dead.

CHAPTER II

MINNETAKI IN THE HANDS OF THE OUTLAWS

For a brief time Roderick believed that life had indeed passed from the body of his young friend. So still did Wabi lie and so terrifying was the strange pallor in his face that the white boy found himself calling on his comrade in a voice filled with choking sobs. The driver of the dog mail dropped on his knees beside the two young hunters. Running his hand under Wabi's thick shirt he held it there for an instant, and said, "He's alive!"

Quickly drawing a small metal flask from one of his pockets he unscrewed the top, and placing the mouthpiece to the Indian youth's lips forced a bit of its contents down his throat. The liquor had almost immediate effect, and Wabigoon opened his eyes, gazed into the rough visage of the courier, then closed them again. There was relief in the courier's face as he pointed to the dogs from Wabinosh House. The exhausted animals were lying stretched upon the snow, their heads drooping between their forefeet. Even the presence of a rival team failed to arouse them from their lethargy. One might have thought that death had overtaken them upon the trail were it not for their panting sides and lolling tongues.

"He's not hurt!" exclaimed the driver, "see the dogs! He's been running—running until he dropped in his tracks!"

The assurance brought but little comfort to Rod. He could feel the tremble of returning life in Wabi's body now, but the sight of the exhausted and bleeding dogs and the memory of his comrade's last words had filled him with a new and terrible fear. What had happened to Minnetaki? Why had the factor's son come all this distance for him? Why had he pursued the mail until his dogs were nearly dead, and he himself had fallen unconscious in his tracks? Was Minnetaki dead? Had the Woongas killed Wabi's beautiful little sister?

Again and again he implored his friend to speak to him, until the courier pushed him back and carried Wabi to the mail sled.

"Hustle up there to that bunch of spruce and build a fire," he commanded. "We've got to get something hot into him, and rub him down, and roll him in furs. This is bad enough, bad enough!"

Rod waited to hear no more, but ran to the clump of spruce to which the courier had directed him. Among them he found a number of birch trees, and stripping off an armful of bark he had a fire blazing upon the snow by the time the dog mail drew up with its unconscious burden. While the driver was loosening Wabi's clothes and bundling him in heavy bearskins Rod added dry limbs to the fire until it threw a warm glow for a dozen paces around. Within a few minutes a pot of ice and snow was melting over the flames and the courier was opening a can of condensed soup.

The deathly pallor had gone from Wabi's face, and Rod, kneeling close beside him, was rejoiced to see the breath coming more and more regularly from between his lips. But even as he rejoiced the other fear grew heavier at his heart. What had happened to Minnetaki? He found himself repeating the question again and again as he watched Wabi slowly returning to life, and, so quickly that it had passed in a minute or two, there flashed through his mind a vision of all that had happened the last few months. For a few moments, as his mind traveled back, he was again in Detroit with his widowed mother; he thought of the day he had first met Wabigoon, the son of an English factor and a beautiful Indian princess, who had come far down into civilization to be educated; of the friendship that had followed, of their weeks and months together in school, and then of those joyous days and nights in which they had planned a winter of thrilling adventure at Wabi's home in the far North.

And what adventures there had been, when, as the Wolf Hunters, he and Wabi and Mukoki had braved the perils of the frozen solitudes! As Wabigoon's breath came more and more regularly he thought of that wonderful canoe trip from the last bit of civilization up into the wilds; of his first sight of moose, the first bear he had killed, and of his meeting with Minnetaki.

His eyes became blurred and his heart grew cold as he thought of what might have happened to her. A vision of the girl swept between him and Wabi's face, in which the glow of life was growing warmer and warmer, a vision of the little half-Indian maiden as he had first seen her, when she came out to meet them in her canoe from Wabinosh House, the sun shining on her dark hair, her cheeks flushed with excitement, her eyes and teeth sparkling in glad welcome to her beloved brother and the white youth of whom she had heard so much—the boy from civilization—Roderick Drew. He remembered how his cap had blown off into the water, how she had rescued it for him. In a flash all that passed after that came before him like a picture; the days that he and Minnetaki had rambled together in the forest, the furious battle in which, single-handed, he had saved her from those fierce outlaw Indians of the North, the Woongas; and after that he thought of the weeks of thrilling adventure they three—Mukoki, Wabigoon and himself—had spent in the wilderness far from the Hudson Bay Post, of their months of trapping, their desperate war with the Woongas, the discovery of the century-old cabin and its ancient skeletons, and their finding of the birch-bark map between the bones of one of the skeleton's fingers, on which, dimmed by age, was drawn the trail to a land of gold.

Instinctively, as for an instant this map came into his mental picture, he thrust a hand into one of his inside pockets to feel that his own copy of that map was there, the map which was to have brought him back into this wilderness a few weeks hence, when they three would set out on the romantic quest for the gold to which the skeletons in the old cabin had given them the key.

The vision left him as he saw a convulsive shudder pass through Wabigoon. In another moment the Indian youth had opened his eyes, and as he looked up into Rod's eager face he smiled feebly. He tried to speak, but words failed him, and his eyes closed again. There was a look of terror in Roderick's face as he turned to the courier, who came to his side. Less than twenty-four hours before he had left Wabigoon in the full strength of his splendid youth at Wabinosh House, a lithe young giant, hardened by their months of adventure, quivering with buoyant life, anxious for the spring that they might meet again to take up another trail into the unexplored North.

And now what a change! The glimpse he had caught of Wabi's bloodshot eyes, the terrible thinness of the Indian youth's face, the chilling lifelessness of his hands, made him shiver with dread. Was it possible that a few short hours could bring about that remarkable transformation? And where was Mukoki, the faithful old warrior from whose guardianship Wabigoon and Minnetaki were seldom allowed to escape?

It seemed an hour before Wabi opened his eyes again, and yet it was only a few minutes. This time Rod lifted him gently in his arms and the courier placed a cup of the hot soup to his lips. The warmth of the liquid put new life into the famished Indian youth. He drank slowly of it at first, then eagerly, and when he had finished the cup he made an effort to sit up.

"I'll take another," he said faintly. "It's mighty good!"

He drank the second cup with even greater relish. Then he sat bolt upright, stretched out his arms, and with his companion's assistance staggered to his feet. His bloodshot eyes burned with a strange excitement as he looked at Rod.

"I was afraid—I wouldn't—catch you!"

"What is it, Wabi? What has happened? You say—Minnetaki—"

"Has been captured by the Woongas. Chief Woonga himself is her captor, and they are taking her into the North. Rod, only you can save her!"

"Only—I—can—save—her?" gasped Rod slowly. "What do you mean?"

"Listen!" cried the Indian boy, clutching him by the arm. "You remember that after our fight with the Woongas and our escape from the chasm we fled to the south, and that the next day, while you were away from camp hunting for some animal that would give us fat for Mukoki's wound, you discovered a trail. You told us that you followed the sledge tracks, and that after a time the party had been met by others on snow-shoes, and that among the imprints in the snow was one that made you think of Minnetaki. When we reached the Post we learned that Minnetaki and two sledges had gone to Kenegami House and at once concluded that those snow-shoe trails were made by Kenegami people sent out to meet her. But they were not! They were made by Woongas!

"One of the guides, who escaped with a severe wound, brought the news to us last night, and the doctor at the Post says that his hurt is fatal and that he will not live another day. Everything depends on you. You and the dying guide are the only two who know where to find the place where the attack was made. It has been thawing for two days and the trail may be obliterated. But you saw Minnetaki's footprints. You saw the snow-shoe trails. You—and you alone—know which way they went!"

Wabi spoke rapidly, excitedly, and then sank down on the sledge, weakened by his exertion.

"We have been chasing you with two teams since dawn," he added, "and pretty nearly killed the dogs. As a last chance we doubled up the teams and I came on alone. I left Mukoki a dozen miles back on the trail."

Rod's blood had turned cold with horror at the knowledge that Minnetaki was in the clutches of Woonga himself. The terrible change in Wabi was no longer a mystery. Both Minnetaki and her brother had told him more than once of the relentless feud waged against Wabinosh House by this bloodthirsty savage and during the last winter he had come into personal contact with it. He had fought, had seen people die, and had almost fallen a victim to Woonga's vengeance.

But it was not of these things that he thought just now. It was of the reason for the feud, and something rose in his throat and choked him until he made no effort to speak. Many years before, George Newsome, a young Englishman, had come to Wabinosh House, and there he had met and fallen in love with a beautiful Indian princess, who loved him in turn, and became his wife. Woonga, chief of a warlike tribe, had been his rival, and when the white man won in the battle for love his fierce heart blazed with the fire of hatred and revenge. From that day the relentless strife against the people of Wabinosh House began. The followers of Woonga turned from trappers and hunters to murderers and outlaws, and became known all over that wilderness country as the Woongas. For years the feud had continued. Like a hawk Woonga watched his opportunities, killing here, robbing there, and always waiting a chance to rob the factor of his wife or children. Only a few weeks before Rod had saved Minnetaki in that terrible struggle in the forest. And now, more hopelessly than before, she had fallen into the clutches of her enemies, and alone with Woonga was being carried into the far North country, into those vast unexplored regions from which she would probably never return!

Rod turned to Wabi, his hands clenched, his eyes blazing.

"I can find the trail, Wabi! I can find the trail—and we'll follow it to the North Pole if we have to! We beat the Woongas in the chasm—we'll beat them now! We'll find Minnetaki if it takes us until doomsday!"

From far back in the forest there came the faint pistol-like cracks of a whip, the distant hallooing of a voice.

For a few moments the three stood listening.

The voice came again.

"It's Mukoki," said Wabigoon, "Mukoki and the other dogs!"

CHAPTER III

ON THE TRAIL OF THE WOONGAS

The cries came nearer, interspersed with the cracking of Mukoki's whip as he urged on the few lagging dogs that Wabi had left with him upon the trail. In another moment the old warrior and his team burst into view and both of the young hunters hurried to meet him. A glance showed Rod that a little longer and Mukoki would have dropped in his tracks, as Wabi had done. The two led their faithful comrade to the heap of bearskins on the mail sled and made him sit there while fresh soup was being made.

"You catch heem," grinned Mukoki joyously. "You catch heem—queek!"

"And pretty nearly killed himself doing it, Muky," added Rod. "Now—" he glanced from one to the other of his companions, "what is the first thing to be done?" "We must strike for the Woonga trail without a moment of unnecessary delay," declared Wabi. "Minutes are priceless, an hour lost or gained may mean everything!"

"But the dogs—"

"You can take mine," interrupted the courier. "There are six of them, all good heavy fellows and not overly bushed. You can add a few of your own and I'll take what's left to drive on the mail. I would advise you to rest for an hour or so and give them and yourselves a good feed. It'll count in the long run."

Mukoki grunted his approval of the driver's words and Rod at once began gathering more fuel for the fire. The temporary camp was soon a scene of the liveliest activity. While the courier unpacked his provisions, Mukoki and Wabigoon assembled the teams and proceeded to select three of the best of their own animals to put in harness with those of the Hudson Bay mail. The dogs from Wabinosh House were wildly famished and at the sight and odor of the great piece of meat which the courier began cutting up for them they set up a snarling and snapping of jaws, and began fighting indiscriminately among themselves until the voices of their human companions were almost drowned in the tumult. A full pound of the meat was given to each dog, and other pieces of it were suspended over beds of coals drawn out from the big fire. Meanwhile Rod was chopping through the thick ice of the lake in search of water.

After a little Wabi came down to join him.

"Our sledge is ready," he said, as Rod stopped to rest for a moment. "We're a little short on grub for nine dogs and three people, but we've got plenty of ammunition. We ought to find something on the trail."

"Rabbits, anyway," suggested Rod, resuming his chopping. A few more strokes, and water gushed through. Filling two pails the boys returned to camp.

The shadows from the sharp pointed cedars of the forest were falling far out upon the frozen lake when the meal was finished, and the sun, sinking early to its rest beyond the homeless solitudes, infused but little warmth as the three hunters prepared to leave. It was only three o'clock, but a penetrating chill was growing in the air. Half an hour more and only a reddish glow would be where the northern sun still shone feebly. In the far North winter night falls with the swiftness of wings; it enshrouds one like a palpable, moving thing, a curtain of gloom that can almost be touched and felt, and so it came now, as the dogs were hitched to their sledge and Rod, Mukoki and Wabigoon bade good-by to the driver of the Hudson Bay mail.

"You'll make the other side in four hours," he called, as Mukoki's cries sent the dogs trotting out upon the lake. "And then—I'd camp!"

Running on ahead Mukoki set the pace and marked the trail. Wabi took the first turn on the sledge, and Rod, who was fresher than either of his comrades, followed close behind. After a little he drew up beside the young Indian and placed a hand on his shoulder as he ran.

"We will reach our old camp—in the plain—to-morrow?" he questioned, between breaths.

"To-morrow," affirmed Wabi. "Mukoki will show us the shortest cut to it. After that, after we reach the camp, everything will depend upon you."

Rod fell behind in the path made by the sledge, and saved his breath. His mind was working as never before in his life. When they reached the camp in which the wounded Mukoki had lain after their escape from the Woongas, could he find the old trail where he had seen Minnetaki's footprints? He was quite sure of himself, and yet he was conscious of an indefinable something growing in him as he noticed more and more what the sun had done that day. Was it nervousness, or fear? Surely he could find the trail, even though it was almost obliterated! But he wished that it had been Mukoki or Wabigoon who had discovered it, either of whom, with the woodcraft instinct born in them, would have gone to it as easily as a fox to the end of a strong trail hidden in autumn leaves. If he did fail—He shuddered, even as he ran, as he thought of the fate that awaited Minnetaki. A few hours before he had been one of the happiest youths in the world. Wabi's lovely little sister, he had believed, was safe at Kenegami House; he had bade adieu to his friends at the Post; every minute after that had taken him nearer to that far city in the South, to his mother, and home. And now so suddenly that he had hardly come to realize the situation he was plunged into what gave promise of being the most thrilling and tragic adventure of his life. A few weeks more, when spring had come, he would have returned to his friends accompanied by his mother, and they three—Mukoki, Wabigoon and he—would have set out on their romantic quest for the lost gold-mine that had been revealed to them by the ancient skeletons in the old cabin. Even as these visions were glowing in his brain there had come the interruption, the signal shots on the lake, the return of the dog mail, and now this race to save the life of Minnetaki!

In his eagerness he ran ahead of the sledge and urged Mukoki into a faster pace. Every ten minutes the one who rode exchanged place with one of the runners, so that there were intervals of rest for each two times an hour. Quickly the red glow over the southwestern forests faded away; the gloom grew thicker; far ahead, like an endless sheet losing itself in a distant smother of blackness, stretched the ice and snow of Lake Nipigon. There was no tree, no rock for guidance over the trackless waste, yet never for an instant did Mukoki or Wabigoon falter. The stars began burning brilliantly in the sky; far away the red edge of the moon rose over this world of ice and snow and forest, throbbing and palpitating like a bursting ball of fire, as one sees it now and then in the glory of the great northern night.

Tirelessly, mile after mile, hour after hour, broken only by the short intervals of rest on the sledge, continued the race across Lake Nipigon. The moon rose higher; the blood in it paled to the crimson glow of the moose flower, and silvered as it climbed into the sky, until the orb hung like a great golden-white disk. In the splendor of it the solitude of ice and snow glistened without end. There was no sound but the slipping of the sledge, the pattering of the dogs' moccasined feet, and now and then a few breathless words spoken by Rod or his companions. It was a little after eight o'clock by Rod's watch when there came a change in the appearance of the lake ahead of them. Wabi, who was on the sledge, was the first to notice it, and he shouted back his discovery to the white youth.

"The forest! We're across!"

The tired dogs seemed to leap into new life at his words, and the leader replied with a whining joyous cry as the odors of balsam and fir came to him. The sharp pinnacles of the forest, reaching up into the night's white glow, grew more and more distinct as the sledge sped on, and five minutes later the team drew up in a huddled, panting bunch on the shore. That day the men and dogs from Wabinosh House had traveled sixty miles.

"We'll camp here!" declared Wabi, as he dropped on the sledge. "We'll camp here— unless you leave me behind!"

Mukoki, tireless to the last, had already found an ax.

"No rest now," he warned, "Too tired! You rest now—build no camp. Build camp—then rest!"

"You're right, Muky," cried Wabi, jumping to his feet with forced enthusiasm. "If I sit down for five minutes I'll fall asleep. Rod, you build a fire. Muky and I will make the shelter."

In less than half an hour the balsam bough shelter was complete, and in front of it roared a fire that sent its light and heat for twenty paces round. From farther back in the forest the three dragged several small logs, and no sooner had they been added to the flames than both Mukoki and Wabigoon wrapped themselves in their furs and burrowed deep into the sweet-scented balsam under the shelter. Rod's experience that day had not been filled with the terrible hardships of his companions, and for some time after they had fallen asleep he sat close to the fire, thinking again of the strangeness with which his fortunes had changed, and watching the flickering firelight as it played in a thousand fanciful figures in the deeper and denser gloom of the forest. The dogs had crept in close to the blazing logs and lay as still as though life no longer animated their tawny bodies. From far away there came the lonely howl of a wolf; a great white man-owl fluttered close to the camp and chortled his crazy, half-human "hello, hello, hello;" the trees cracked with the tightening frost, but neither wolf howl nor frost nor the ghostly visitant's insane voice aroused those who were sleeping.

An hour passed and still Rod sat by the fire; his rifle lying across his knees. His imagination had painted a thousand pictures in that time. Never for an instant had his mind ceased to work. Somewhere in that great wilderness there was another camp-fire that night, and in that camp Minnetaki was a captive. Some indefinable sensation seemed to creep into him, telling him that she was awake, and that she was thinking of her friends. Was it a touch of sleep, or that wonderful thing called mental telepathy, that wrought the next picture in his brain? It came with startling vividness. He saw the girl beside a fire. Her beautiful hair, glistening black in the firelight, hung in a heavy braid over her shoulder; her eyes were staring wildly into the flames, as if she were about to leap into them, and back of her so close that he might have touched her, was a figure that sent a chill of horror through him. It was Woonga, the outlaw chief! He was talking, his red face was fiendish, he stretched out a hand!

With a cry that startled the dogs Rod sprang to his feet. He was shivering as if in a chill. Had he dreamed? Or was it something more than a dream? He thought of the vision that had come to him weeks before in the mysterious chasm, the vision of the dancing skeletons, and which had revealed the secret of the old cabin and the lost gold. In vain he tried to shake off his nervousness and his fear. Why had Woonga reached out his hands for Minnetaki? He worked to free himself of the weight that had fallen on him, stirred the fire until clouds of sparks shot high up into the gloom of the trees, and added new fuel.

Then he sat down again, and for the twentieth time since leaving Wabinosh House drew from his pocket the map that was to have led them on their search for gold when he returned with his mother. It was a vision that had guided him to the discovery of this precious map, and the knowledge of it made him more uneasy now. A few moments before he had seen Minnetaki as plainly as though she had been with him there beside the fire; he fancied that he might almost have sent a bullet through the Indian's chief face as he reached out his long arms toward the girl.

He stirred the fire again, awakened one of the dogs to keep him company, and then went in to lie down between Mukoki and Wabigoon in an attempt at slumber. During the hours that followed he secured only short snatches of sleep. He dreamed, dreamed constantly of Minnetaki whenever he lost consciousness. Now he saw her before the fire, as he had seen her in his vision; again, she was struggling in the Woonga's powerful grasp. At one time the strife between the two—the young girl and the powerful savage—became terrible for him to behold, and at last he saw the Indian catch her in his arms and disappear into the blackness of the forest.

This time when he wakened Rod made no further effort to sleep. It was only a little past midnight. His companions had obtained four hours of rest. In another hour he would arouse them. Quietly he began making preparations for breakfast, and fed the dogs. At half-past one o'clock he shook Wabigoon by the shoulder.

"Get up!" he cried, as the Indian youth sat erect. "It's time to go!"

He tried to suppress his nervousness when Mukoki and Wabi joined him beside the fire. He determined not to let them know of his visions, for there was gloom enough among them as it was. But he would hurry. He was the first to get through with breakfast, the first to set to work among the dogs, and when Mukoki started out at the head of the team through the forest he was close beside him, urging him to greater speed by his own endeavors.

"How far are we from the camp, Mukoki?" he asked.

"Four hour—twent' mile," replied the old pathfinder.

"Twenty miles. We ought to make it by dawn."

Mukoki made no answer, but quickened his pace as the cedar and balsam forest gave place to an open plain which stretched for a mile or two ahead of them. For an hour longer the moon continued to light up the wilderness; then, with its descent lower and lower into the west, the gloom began to thicken, until only the stars were left to guide the pursuers. Even these were beginning to fade when Mukoki halted the panting team on the summit of a mountainous ridge, and pointed into the north.

"The plains!"

For several minutes the three stood silent, gazing out into the gloom of the vast solitudes that swept unbroken to Hudson Bay. Again Rod's blood was thrilled with the romance of what lay at his feet and far beyond, thrilled with the romance and mystery of that land of the wild which reached for hundreds of miles into the North, and into which the foot of the white man had as yet scarce left its imprint.

Before him, enveloped now in the deep gloom of the northern night, slept a vast unexplored world, a land whose story the passing of ages had left unrevealed. What tragedies of nature had its silent fastnesses beheld? What treasure did they hold? Half a century or more ago the men whose skeletons they had found in the old cabin had braved the perils of those trackless solitudes, and somewhere hundreds of miles out in that black gloom they had found gold, the gold that had fallen as an inheritance to them in the discovery of the old birch-bark map. And somewhere, somewhere out there was Minnetaki!

Across the plain at their feet the three adventurers had raced for their lives from the bloodthirsty Woongas only a week or so before; now they crossed it a second time and at even greater speed, for then they had possessed no dogs. At the end of another hour Mukoki no longer traveled faster than a walk. His eyes were constantly on the alert. Occasionally he would stop the dogs and strike off to the right or the left of the trail alone. He spoke no word to his companions, and neither Rod nor Wabigoon offered a suggestion. They knew, without questioning, that they were approaching their old camp, and just as the experienced hunter makes no sign or sound while his dog is nosing out a half-lost trail so they held back while Mukoki, the most famous pathfinder in all those regions, led them slowly on. The last of the stars went out. For a time the blackness of the night grew deeper; then, in the southeast, came the first faint streak of dawn. Day is born as suddenly as it dies in these regions, and it was soon light enough for Mukoki to resume his trail at a trot. A few minutes more and a clump of balsam and spruce loomed up out of the plain ahead of them. Neither Rod nor Wahigoon recognized it until the old warrior halted the dogs close in its shadows and they saw the look of triumph in his face.

"The camp!" breathed Wabi.

"The camp!"

Trembling, his voice quivering with suppressed excitement, the Indian youth turned to Roderick Drew.

"Rod—it's all up to you!"

Mukoki, too, had come close to his side.

"There—camp!" he whispered. "Now—where Minnetaki's trail?"

The old warrior's eyes were blazing.

"Where?"

A dozen paces away was the balsam shelter they had built. But that was all. Not a track was left in the snow. The warm sun had obliterated every sign of their presence of a short time before!

If their own trail was gone what could he hope to find of Minnetaki's dainty foot-prints?

Deep down in his heart Rod prayed for guidance in this moment of terrible doubt.

CHAPTER IV

ROD FOLLOWS THE MAN-FOOTED BEAR

"I must wait until it is lighter," he said. He tried to control himself, to fortify himself with the assurance which he no longer felt.

"We will have breakfast," suggested Wabi. "We have cold meat and there will be no need of a fire."

Finishing before the others, Rod grasped his rifle and walked out from among the trees. Wabi made a movement as if to follow, but Mukoki held him back. There was a shrewd light in his eyes.

"He do better—alone," he warned.

The red glow of the sun was rising above the forest and Rod could now see far about him. He had come out from the cedars, like this, on the afternoon that he had gone to hunt and had found Minnetaki's trail. A mile away he saw the snow-covered ridge where he had hunted for moose. That ridge was his first guide, and he hurried toward it while Mukoki and Wabigoon followed far behind him with the dogs and the sledge. He was breathless when he reached the top. Eagerly he gazed into the North. It was in that direction he had gone on the afternoon of his discovery of the strange trail. But nothing that he recognized met his eyes now, no familiar landmark or tree to guide him again over his wandering footsteps of that day. Vainly he sought along the ridge for some slight sign of his former presence there. But everything was gone. The sun had destroyed his last hope.

He was glad that Mukoki and Wabigoon were at the foot of the ridge, for he knew that his despair almost brought tears to his eyes, Minnetaki's fate was in his hands—and he had failed. He dreaded to tell his companions, to let them see his face. For once in his life, though he was as courageous a youth as ever lived, Roderick Drew almost wished that he was dead.

Suddenly, as in their hopeless search for some familiar object Rod's eyes traveled again over the endless waste of snow, he saw, far away, something that glittered in the morning sun like a pane of glass, and from his lips there fell a low exultant cry. He remembered now that he had seen that strange gleam before, that he had gone straight to it from the ridge and had found it to be a sheet of crystal ice frozen to the side of a rock from above which the water of a spring gushed forth. Without waiting for his companions he hurried down the ridge and sped like a deer across the narrow plain at its foot. A five-minute run brought him to the rock, and for a moment he paused, his heart almost choking him in its excitement. Just beyond this he had first encountered the strange trail. There were no signs of it left in the snow, but he saw other things which led him on: a huge rock thrusting itself out of the chaos of white, a dead poplar which stood in his path, and at last, half a mile ahead, the edge of a dense forest.

He turned and waved his arms wildly to Mukoki and Wabigoon, who were far behind. Then he ran on, and when he reached the forest he waved his arms again, and his joy was flung back in a thrilling shout to his comrades. There was the log on which Minnetaki had been forced to sit while awaiting the pleasure of her savage captors; he found the very spot where her footprint had been in the snow, close to a protruding stub! The outlaw Indians and their captives had rested here for a brief spell, and had built a fire, and so many feet had beaten the snow about it that their traces still remained.

He pointed to these signs as Mukoki and Wabigoon joined him.

For several minutes no one of the three spoke a word. Crouched over until his eyes were within a foot of the snow the old pathfinder examined every inch of the little clearing in which the Woongas had built their fire, and when at last he drew himself erect his face betrayed the utmost astonishment.

The boys saw that in those faint marks in the snow he had discovered something of unusual if not startling significance.

"What is it, Muky?" asked the young Indian.

Mukoki made no reply, but returning to the charred remains of the fire he again fell upon his hands and knees and repeated his strange scrutiny of the snow even more closely than before. When he arose a second time the astonishment had grown deeper in his face.

"Only six!" he exclaimed. "Two guides from Post—four Woongas!"

"But the wounded driver told us that there were at least a dozen Woongas in the attacking party," said Wabi.

The old warrior chuckled, and for a moment his face twisted itself into a ludicrous grimace.

"Driver lie!" he declared. "He run when fight begin. Shot in back while heem run!"

He pointed into the cold depths of the forest.

"No sun there! Follow trail easy!"

There was no uneasiness in Mukoki's manner now. His eyes gleamed, but it was with the fire of battle and resolution, not with excitement. Once before Rod had seen that look in the old warrior's face, when they two had fought to save Wabigoon's life as they were now about to fight to save Minnetaki. And he knew what it meant. Cautiously they penetrated the forest, their eyes and ears alert, and, as Mukoki had predicted, the trail of the retreating savages was quite distinct. They had taken both of the captured sledges, and Rod knew that on one of these Minnetaki was being carried. Hardly had the three progressed a hundred paces when Mukoki, who was in the lead, stopped short with a huge grunt. Squarely across the trail lay the body of a dead man. A glance at the upturned face showed that it was one of the two drivers from Wabinosh House.

"Head split," said Mukoki, as he led the team around the body. "Shot, mebby—then killed with ax."

The dogs sniffed and cringed as they passed the slain man, and Rod shuddered. Involuntarily he thought of what might have happened to Minnetaki, and he noticed that after passing this spectacle of death Mukoki doubled his speed. For an hour the pursuit continued without interruption. The Woongas were traveling in a narrow trail, single file, with the two sledges between their number. At the end of that hour the three came upon the remains of another camp-fire near which were built two cedar-bough shelters. Here the tracks in the snow were much fresher; in places they seemed to have been but lately made. Still there were no evidences of the captured girl. The boys could see that Mukoki himself had found no explanation for the sudden freshness of the trail and for the absence of Minnetaki's footprints among the tracks. Again and again the shrewd old pathfinder went over the camp. Not a sign escaped his eyes, not a mark or a broken stick but that was examined by him. Rod knew that Minnetaki's capture must have occurred at least three days before, and yet the tracks about this camp were not more than a day old, if they were that. What did it mean?

The very mystery of the thing filled him with a nameless fear. Why had not the outlaw Woongas continued their flight? Why this delay so near the scene of their crime? He glanced at Wabi, but the Indian youth was as bewildered as himself. In his eyes, too, there was the gleam of a fear which he could not have named.

Mukoki was beside the charred remains of the fire. He had buried his hand deep among them, and when he rose be made a sign toward Rod's watch.

"Eight o'clock, Mukoki."

"Woonga here las' night," declared the old Indian slowly. "Leave camp four hour ago!"

What did it mean?

Had Minnetaki been hurt, so dangerously hurt that her captors had not dared to move her?

Rod asked himself no more questions. But he was trembling. And Mukoki and Wabigoon went on with strange, unnatural faces and breathed not the whisper of a word between them. The mystery was beyond them all. But one thing they realized, whatever had happened they were close upon the heels of the savages. And each step brought them nearer, for with every mile the freshness of the trail increased. Then came another great surprise.

The trail divided!

At the edge of a small opening the Indians had separated themselves into two parties. The trail of one sledge led into the northeast, that of the other into the northwest!

With which sledge was Minnetaki? They looked at one another in bewilderment.

Mukoki pointed to the trail into the northeast.

"We must fin' sign—sign of Minnetaki. You take that—I take this!"

Rod started off at a dog trot over the easternmost trail. At the farther side of the opening, where the sledge had plunged into a clump of hazel, he suddenly stopped, and for a second time that morning a thrilling cry escaped his lips. On a projecting thorny twig, glistening full in the sun, there fluttered a long, silken strand of hair. He reached out for it, but Wabi caught his hand, and in another moment Mukoki had joined them. Gently he took the raven tress between his fingers, his deep-set eyes glaring like red coals of fire. It was a strand of Minnetaki's beautiful hair, not for a moment did one of them doubt that; but what held them most, what increased the horror in their eyes, was the quantity of it! Suddenly Mukoki gave it a gentle pull and the tress slipped free of the twig.

In the next breath he uttered the only expression of supreme disgust in his vocabulary a long-drawn, hissing sound which he used only in those moments when his command of English was entirely inadequate to the situation.

"Minnetaki on other sledge!"

He showed the end of the strand to his young companions.

"See—hair been cut! No pulled out by, twig. Woonga hang heem there—make us think wrong."

He waited for no reply, but darted back to the other trail, with Wabi and Rod close behind him. A quarter of a mile farther on the old pathfinder paused and pointed in exultant silence at a tiny footprint close beside the path of the sledge. At almost regular intervals now there appeared this sign of Minnetaki's moccasin. Her two guards were running ahead of the sledge, and it was apparent to the pursuers that Wabi's sister was taking advantage of her opportunities to leave these signs behind for those whom she knew would make an attempt at her rescue. And yet, as they left farther and farther behind them the trail which ran into the northeast, an inexplicable feeling of uneasiness began to steal over Rod. What if Mukoki had made a mistake? His confidence in the old warrior's judgment and sagacity was usually absolute, but it occurred to him, like an ugly humor to stir up his fears, that if the Woongas could cut off a bit of the girl's hair they could also take off one of her shoes! Several times he was on the point of giving audible voice to his suspicions but refrained from doing so when he saw the assurance with which both Wabi and Mukoki followed the trail.

Finally he could hold himself no longer.

"Wabi, I'm going back," he cried softly, forging alongside his companion. "I'm going back and follow the other trail. If I don't find anything in a mile or so I'll return on the double-quick and overtake you!"

Wabi's efforts to dissuade him were futile, and a few minutes later Rod was again at the clearing. What presentiment was it that caused his heart to beat faster and his breath to come in tense excitement as he stole through the bushes where they had found the silken tress of hair? What something was it, away down in his soul, that kept urging him on and on, even after he had gone a mile, and then two miles, in fruitless search? Rod could not have answered these questions had he stopped to ask them of himself. He was not superstitious. He did not believe in dreams. And yet each moment, without apparent reason added to his conviction that Mukoki had made a mistake, and that Minnetaki was on the sledge ahead of him.

The country into which he was penetrating grew wilder. Rocky ridges rose before him, split by rifts and gullies through which the water must have rushed in torrents in the spring. He listened, and proceeded more cautiously; and through his mind there flashed a memory of his thrilling exploration of the mysterious chasm of a few weeks before, when, in his lonely night camp, he had dreamed of the skeletons. He was thinking of this when he came around the end of a huge rock which lay as big as a house in his path. Upon the snow, almost at his feet, was a sight that froze the blood in his veins. For the second time that day he gazed upon the distorted features of a dead man. Squarely across the trail, as the other had lain, was the body of an Indian, his arms outstretched, his twisted face turned straight up to the clear sky, the snow about his head glistening a sickening red in the sun. For a full minute Rod gazed in silent horror on the scene. There was no sign of a struggle, there were no footprints in the snow. The man had been killed while upon the sledge, and the only mark he had made was when he had fallen off.

Who had killed him?

Had Minnetaki saved herself by taking her captor's life?

For a moment Rod was almost convinced that this was so. He examined the stains in the snow and found that they were still damp and unfrozen. He was sure that the tragedy had occurred less than an hour before. More cautiously, and yet swifter than before, he followed the trail of the sledge, his rifle held in readiness for a shot at any moment. The path became wilder and in places it seemed almost inaccessible. But between the tumbled mass of rock the sledge had found its way, its savage driver not once erring in his choice of the openings ahead. Gradually the trail ascended until it came to the summit of a huge ridge. Hardly had Rod reached the top when another trail cut across that of the sledge.

Deeply impressed in the softening snow were the footprints of a big bear!

The first warm sunshine, thought Rod, had aroused the beast from his winter sleep, and he was making a short excursion from his den. From where the bear had crossed the trail the sledge turned abruptly in the direction from which the bear had come.

Without giving a thought to his action, Rod began his descent of the ridge in the trail made by the bear, at the same time keeping his eyes fixed upon the sledge track and the distant forest. At the foot of the ridge the great trunk of a fallen tree lay in his path, and as he went to climb over it he stopped, a cry of amazement stifling itself in his throat. Over that tree the bear had scrambled, and upon it, close to the spot where the animal had brushed off the snow in his passage, was the imprint of a human hand!

For a full minute Rod stood as motionless as if he had been paralyzed, scarcely breathing in his excitement. The four fingers and thumb of the hand had left their impressions with startling clearness. The fingers were long and delicately slender, the palm narrow. The imprint had assuredly not been made by the hand of a man!

Recovering himself, Rod looked about him. There were no marks in the snow except those of the bear. Was it possible that he was mistaken? He scrutinized the mysterious handprint again. As he gazed an uncanny chill crept through him, and when he raised his head he knew that he was trembling in spite of his efforts to control himself. Turning about he swiftly followed the trail to the top of the ridge, recrossed the sledge track, and descended again into the wildness of the gorge on the other side. He had not progressed twenty rods when without a sound he dropped behind a rock. He had seen no movement ahead of him. He had heard nothing. Yet in that moment he was thrilled as never before in his life.

For the bear trail had ceased.

And ahead of him, instead of the tracks of a beast, there continued *the footprints of a man*!

CHAPTER V

ROD'S FIGHT FOR LIFE

It was some time before Roderick moved from his concealment behind the rock. It was not fear that held him there, but a knowledge within him that he needed to think, to collect his senses as he would have expressed it if Wabi had been with him. For a brief spell he was stunned by the succession of surprises which he had encountered, and he felt that now, if ever in his life, he needed control of himself. He did not attempt to solve the mystery of the trail beyond the fact that it was not made by a bear and that the handprint on the log was not made by a man. But he was certain of one thing. In some way Minnetaki was associated with both.

When he continued his pursuit he made his way with extreme caution. At each new turn in the trail he fell behind some rock or clump of bushes and scanned the gorge as far as he could see ahead of him. But each moment these distances of observation became shorter. The ridge on his left became almost a sheer wall; on his right a second ridge closed in until the gorge had narrowed to a hundred feet in width, choked by huge masses of rock thrown there in some mighty upheaval of past ages. It was very soon apparent to Rod that the mysterious person whom he was pursuing was perfectly at home in the lonely chasm. As straight as a drawn whip-lash his trail led from one break in the rocky chaos to another. Never did he err. Once the tracks seemed to end squarely against a broad face of rock, but there the young hunter found a cleft in the granite wall scarcely wider than his body, through which he cautiously wormed his way. Where this cleft opened into the chasm again the fugitive had rested for a few moments, and had placed some burden upon the snow at his feet. A single glance disclosed what this burden had been, for in the snow was that same clearly-defined impression of a human hand!

There was no longer a doubt in Roderick's mind. He was on the trail of Minnetaki's captor, and the outlaw was carrying his victim in his arms! Minnetaki was injured! Perhaps she was dead. The fear gripped at his heart until he looked again at the imprint in the snow—the widely spread fingers, the flat, firm palm. Only a living hand would have left its mark in that manner.

As on that autumn day in the forest, when he had fought for Minnetaki's life, so now all hesitation and fear left him. His blood leaped with anticipation rather than excitement, and he was eager for the moment when he would once more throw his life in the balance in behalf of Wabi's sister. He was determined to take advantage of the Woonga fighting code and fire upon his enemy from ambush if the opportunity offered, but at the same time he had no dread at the thought of engaging in a closer struggle if this should be necessary. He looked well to his rifle, loosened his big army revolver in its holster, and saw that his hunting-knife did not stick in its scabbard. A short distance from the cleft in the wall of rock the outlaw had rested again; and this time, when he continued his flight, Minnetaki had walked beside him.

A peculiarity in the new trail struck Rod, and for some moments he was at a loss to account for it. One of the girl's dainty feet left its moccasin imprint very distinctly; the mark of the other was no more than a formless blotch in the snow. Then the youth thought of the footprints that were leading on Mukoki and Wabigoon, and despite his desperate situation he could not repress a smile. He had been right. The Woongas had taken off one of Minnetaki's moccasins and were using it to make a false trail into the northwest. Those formless tracks ahead of him meant that one of the Indian maiden's feet was wrapped with a bit of cloth or fur to protect it from the cold.

Rod soon perceived that the flight of the outlaw and his captive was now much more rapid, and he quickened his own pace. The chasm grew wilder. At times it appeared impassable, but always the trail of the fugitives led straight to some hidden cleft through which the boy followed, holding his breath in tense expectancy of what might happen at any instant.

Suddenly Rod stopped. From ahead of him he was sure that he had heard a sound. He scarcely breathed while he listened. But there came no repetition of the noise. Had some animal, a fox or a wolf, perhaps, set a stone rolling down one of the precipitous walls of the chasm? He went on slowly, listening, watching. A few paces more and he stopped again. There was a faint, suspicious odor in the air; a turn around the end of a huge mass of rock and his nostrils were filled with it, the pungent odor of smoke mingled with the sweet scent of burning cedar!

There was a fire ahead of him. More than that, it was not a gunshot away!

For a space of sixty seconds he stood still, nerving himself for the final step. His resolution was made. He would creep upon the outlaw and shoot him down. There would be no warning, no quarter, no parley. Foot by foot he advanced, as stealthily as a fox. The odor of smoke came to him more plainly; over his head he saw thin films of it floating lazily up the chasm. It came from beyond another of those walls of rock which seemed to bar his way, creeping up over it as though the fire were just on the other side. With his rifle half to his shoulder Rod stole through the break in this wall. At its farther end he peered out cautiously, exposing his face an inch at a time. Wider and wider became his vision. There was no trail ahead. The outlaw and his captive were behind the rock!

With his rifle now full to his shoulder Rod stepped boldly forth and whirled to the left. Twenty feet away, almost entirely concealed among the tumbled masses of boulders, was a small cabin. About it there were no signs of life with the exception of a thin wreath of smoke rising like a ghostly spiral up the side of the chasm wall; from it there came no sound. Rod's index finger quivered on the trigger of his rifle. Should he wait— until the outlaw came forth? Half a minute he stood there, a minute, two minutes, and still he heard nothing, saw nothing. He advanced a step, then another, and still another, until he saw the open door of the cabin. And as he stood there, his rifle leveled, there came to him a faint, sobbing cry, a cry that reached out and caught him like a strong hand and brought him in a single desperate leap to the door itself.

Inside the cabin was Minnetaki, alone! She was crouched upon the floor, her beautiful hair tumbling in disheveled masses over her shoulders and into her lap, her face, as white as death, staring wildly at the youth who had appeared like an apparition before her.

In an instant Rod was at her side, upon his knees. For that brief moment he had lost his caution, and only a terrible cry from the girl turned him back again, half upon his feet, to the door. Standing there, about to spring upon him, was one of the most terrifying figures he had ever seen. In a flash he saw the huge form of an Indian, a terrible face, the gleam of an uplifted knife. In such a crisis one's actions are involuntary, machine-like, as if life itself, hovering by a thread, protects itself in its own manner without thought or reasoning on the part of the human creature it animates. Rod neither thought nor reasoned; without any motive on his own part, he flung himself face downward upon the cabin floor. And the move saved him. With a guttural cry the savage leaped toward him, struck out with his knife and missed, stumbled over the boy's prostrate form and fell beside him.

Months of hardship and adventure in the wilderness had made Rod as lithe as a forest cat, his muscles like steel. Without rising he flung himself upon his enemy, his own knife raised in gleaming death above the savage's breast. But the Woonga was as quick. Like a flash he struck up with one of his powerful arms and the force of the blow that was descending upon him fell to the earth floor. In another instant his free arm had encircled Rod's neck, and for a few brief moments the two were locked in a crushing embrace, neither being able to use the weapon in his hand without offering an advantage to the other.

In that respite, which only death could follow, Rod's brain worked with the swiftness of fire. He was lying face downward upon his enemy; the Woonga was flat upon his back, the latter's knife hand stretched out behind his head with Rod's knife hand locking it. For either to strike a blow both of their fighting hands must be freed. In the first instant of that freedom, the savage, with his arm already extended, could deliver a blow sooner than his antagonist, who would have to raise his arm as well as strike. In other words, by the time Rod's knife was poised his enemy's would be buried in his breast. With a curious thrill the white youth saw the fearful odds against him in their position. If he remained clutched in the Indian's embrace there would be only one end. He would die, and Minnetaki would be more than ever in the power of her captor.

There was only one chance now, and that was to break away, at least to free himself enough to get hold of his revolver. He was nerving himself for the strain when, turning his head a trifle sidewise, he saw Minnetaki. The girl had risen to her feet, and Rod saw that her hands were bound behind her. She, too, realized the disadvantage of Rod's position in the contest, and now with a thrilling cry she sprang to the outlaw's head and stepped with all her weight upon his extended arm.

"Quick, Rod—quick!" she cried. "Strike! Strike!"

With a terrible yell the powerful savage wrenched his arm free; in a last superhuman effort he swung his knife upward as Rod's blade sank to the hilt in his breast, and the blow fell with a sickening thud under Rod's arm. With a sharp cry the young hunter staggered to his feet, and the Indian's knife fell from him, red with blood. Making an effort to control himself he picked up the knife and loosed the captive girl's arms.

There came over him then a strange dizziness, a weakness in his limbs. He was conscious that his head was sinking, and he knew, too, that a pair of arms was about him, and that from what seemed to be a great, great distance a voice was calling to him, calling his name. And then he seemed to be sinking into a deep and painless sleep.

When he regained consciousness his eyes were first turned to the door, which was still open, and through which he caught the white gleam of the snow. A hand was pressed gently upon his face.

"Rod—"

Minnetaki spoke in a whisper, a whisper that trembled with gladness, with relief. Rod smiled. Weakly he lifted a hand and touched the sweet, white face above him.

"I'm glad to see you—Minnetaki—" he breathed.

The girl quickly put a cup of cold water to his lips.

"You mustn't try to move," she said softly, her eyes glowing. "It isn't a very bad wound, and I've dressed it nicely. But you mustn't move—or talk—or it may begin bleeding again."

"But I'm so glad to see you, Minnetaki," persisted the youth. "You don't know how disappointed I was to find you gone when we returned to Wabinosh House from our hunting trip. Wabi and Mukoki—"

"Sh-h-h-h!"

Minnetaki placed her hand upon his lips.

"You must keep quiet, Roderick. Don't you know how curious I am to know how you are here? But you must not tell me—now. Let me do the talking. Will you? Please!"

Involuntarily the young girl's eyes left his face, and Rod, weakly following her gaze, saw that a blanket had been spread over a huddled heap in the middle of the floor. He shuddered, and feeling the sudden tremor in his hand Minnetaki turned to him quickly, her cheeks whiter than before, but her eyes shining like stars.

"It is Woonga," she whispered. In her voice was a thrilling tremble.
"It is Woonga, and he is dead!"

Rod understood the look in her face now. Woonga, the Nemesis of her people, the outlaw chief who had sworn vengeance on the house of Wabinosh, and whose murderous hand had hovered for years like a threatening cloud over the heads of the factor and his wife and children, was dead! And he, Roderick Drew, who once before had saved Minnetaki's life, had killed him. In his weakness and pain he smiled, and said,

"I am glad, Minne—"

He did not finish. There had come a stealthy, crumbling step to the door, and in another moment Mukoki and Wabigoon were in the little cabin.

CHAPTER VI

THE SHADOW OF DEATH

Rod was hardly conscious of what passed during the next half-hour. The excitement of the sudden entrance of Minnetaki's brother and the old Indian set his head reeling, and he sank back upon the blankets, from which he had partly raised himself, fainting and weak. The last that he heard was Minnetaki's warning voice, and then he felt something cool upon his face. It seemed a long time before he heard sound again, and when he stirred himself, struggling toward consciousness, there came a whisper in his ear urging him to be quiet. It was Minnetaki, and he obeyed.

After a little he heard low voices, and then movement, and opened his eyes. He could feel Minnetaki's gentle hand stroking his face and hair, as if weaning him to sleep, and at his feet he saw Mukoki, the old warrior, crouching like a lynx, his beady eyes glaring at him. The glare fascinated Roderick. He had seen it in Mukoki's eyes before, when the Indian believed that injury had come to those he loved; and when the white boy saw it now, bent upon himself, he knew that he, too, had become more than a friend to this savage pathfinder of the wilderness. Minnetaki's caressing hand and the fearful anxiety in the crouching posture of the old hunter thrilled him, and two words fell from his lips before they knew that he had come back into life.

"Hello, Muky!"

Instantly the old Indian was at his side, kneeling there silent, trembling, his face twitching with joy, his eyes gleaming, and where he had crouched a moment before there came Wabigoon, smiling down upon Rod in his own bursting happiness, which was only held in check by Minnetaki's hand and the almost inaudible "Sh-h-h-h!" that fell from her lips.

"You right—me wrong," the white boy heard Mukoki saying. "You save Minnetaki—kill Woonga. Very much dam'—dam'—dam'—brave man!"

Mukoki was pressed back by Wabi's sister before he could say more, and a cool drink of spring water was placed to Roderick's lips. He felt feverish and the water gave him new strength. He turned his face to Minnetaki, and she smiled at him. Then he saw that the dead outlaw had been removed from the cabin. When he made an effort to raise himself a little the girl helped him, and rolled a blanket under his shoulders.

"You're not so badly hurt as I thought you were, Rod," she said. "That is, you're not dangerously hurt. Mukoki has dressed your wound, and you will be better soon." Wabigoon, coming nearer, put both arms around his lovely little sister and kissed her again and again.

"Rod, you're a hero!" he cried softly, gripping his comrade's hand.
"God bless you!"

Rod blushed, and to restrain further effusions closed his eyes. During the next quarter of an hour Minnetaki prepared some coffee and meat, while both Mukoki and Wabi cared for the sledge-dogs outside.

"To-morrow, if you are stronger, we're going to take you on to Kenegami House," the girl said to him. "Then you can tell me all about your adventures during the winter. Wabi has told me just enough about your battles with the Indians and about the old skeletons and the lost gold-mine to set me wild. Oh, I wish you would take me with you on your hunt for gold!"

"By George, I wish we could!" exclaimed Rod with enthusiasm. "Coax Wabi, Minnetaki—coax him hard."

"You'll coax him, too, won't you, Rod? But then, I don't suppose it will do any good. And father and mother wouldn't listen to it for a moment. All of them are so afraid that some harm is going to befall me. That's why they sent me from Wabinosh House just before you boys returned. You see the Indians were more hostile than ever, and they thought I would be safer at Kenegami House. How I do wish they'd let me go! I'd love to hunt bears, and wolves, and moose, and help you find the gold. Please coax him hard, Roderick!"

And that very day, when he was strong enough to sit up, Rod did plead with his half-Indian comrade that Minnetaki might be allowed to accompany them. But Wabi stanchly refused even to consider the proposition, and Mukoki, when he learned of the girl's desire, grinned and chuckled in his astonishment for the next half-hour.

"Minnetaki ver' brave—ver' brave girl," he confided to Rod, "but she die up there, I guess so! You want Minnetaki die?"

Rod assured him that he did not, and the subject was dropped.

That day and night in the old cabin was one of the pleasantest within Rod's memory, despite the youth's wound. A cheerful fire of dry pine and poplar burned in the stone fireplace, and when Minnetaki announced that the evening meal was ready Rod was for the first time allowed to leave his bunk. For the greater part of the day Wabi and Mukoki had searched in the chasm and along the mountains for signs of the outlaw Indian's band, but their search had revealed nothing to arouse their fears. As mysterious and unaccountable as the fact seemed, there was no doubt that the old cabin was a retreat known only to Woonga himself, and as the four sat in the warm glow of the fire, eating and drinking, the whole adventure was gone over again and again until there seemed no part of it left in doubt. Minnetaki described her capture and explained the slowness of their flight after the massacre. Woonga was ill and had refused to move far from the scene of the slaughter until he had fully regained his strength.

"But why did Woonga kill the Indian back on the trail?" asked Rod.

Minnetaki shuddered as she thought of the terrible scene that had been enacted before her eyes.

"I heard them quarreling," she said, "but I couldn't understand. I know that it was about me. We had gone but a short distance after the sledges separated when Woonga, who was ahead of me, turned about and shot the other in the breast. It was terrible! And then he drove on as coolly as though nothing had happened."

"I'm curious to know how he used the bear's feet," exclaimed Rod.

"They were huge pads into which he slipped his feet, moccasins and all," explained Minnetaki. "He told me that the dogs would go on to Kenegami House, and that if pursuers followed us they would follow the sledge trail and never give a thought to the bear tracks."

Mukoki chuckled deep down in his throat.

"He no fool Rod," he said. "Nobody fool Rod!"

"Especially when he's on Minnetaki's trail," laughed Wabi happily.

"Wasn't it Rod who discovered the secret of the lost gold, after you had given up all hope?" retorted Minnetaki.

The lost gold!

How those three words, falling clearly from the girl's lips, thrilled the hearts of Mukoki and the young adventurers. Night had closed in, and only the fitful flashes of the fire illumined the interior of the old cabin. The four had finished eating, and as they drew themselves close about the fire there fell a strange silence among them. The lost gold. Rod gazed across at Wabigoon, whose bronzed face was half hid in the dancing shadows, and then at Mukoki, whose wrinkled visage shone like dull copper as he stared like some watchful animal into the flame glow. But it was Minnetaki who sent the blood in a swift rush of joy and pride through his veins. He caught her eyes upon him, shining like stars from out of the gloom, and he knew that she was looking at him in that way because he was her hero.

For many minutes no one broke the stillness. The fire burned down, and with its slow dying away the gloom in the corners of the old cabin thickened, and the faces became more and more like ghostly shadows, until they reminded Rod of his first vision of the ancient skeletons in that other old cabin many miles away. Then came Wabigoon's voice, as he stirred the coals and added fresh fuel.

"Yes, it was Rod. This is the map he found, Minnetaki."

He kneeled close beside his sister and drew forth his copy of the precious secret which the skeletons had guarded. With a little cry of excitement the girl took the map in her hands, and step by step, adventure by adventure, was gone over the thrilling story of the Wolf Hunters, until the late hours of night had changed into the first of morning. Twice did Minnetaki insist on having repeated to her the story of Rod's wild adventure in the mysterious chasm, and when he came to the terrors of that black night and its strange sounds Rod felt a timid little hand come close to him, and as Wabigoon continued the narration, and told of the map in the skeleton hand, and of the tale of murder and tragedy it revealed, Minnetaki's breath came in quick, tense eagerness.

"And you are going back in the spring?" she asked.

"In the spring," replied Rod.

Again Wabigoon urged Rod, as he had done at the Post, to send down to civilization for his mother instead of going for her himself. Time would be saved, he argued. They could set out on their search for the gold within a few weeks. But Rod was firm.

"It would not be fair to mother," he declared. "I must go home first, even if I have to arrange for a special sledge at Kenegami House to take me down to civilization."

But even while he was stoutly declaring what it was his intention to do, fate was stealthily at work weaving another of her webs of destiny for Roderick Drew, and his friends' anxious eyes saw the first signs of it when they bade him good night. For fever had laid its hand on the white youth, the fever that foreshadows death unless a surgeon is near, the fever of a wound going bad. Even Mukoki, graduated by Nature, taught by half a century's battle with life in this great desolation of the North, knew that his own powers were now of no avail.

So Roderick was bundled in blankets, and the race for life to Kenegami House was begun. It was a race of which Rod could only guess the import, for he did not know that Death was running a fierce pursuit behind. Many days and nights of delirium followed. One morning he seemed to awaken from a terrible dream, in which he was constantly burning and roasting, and when he opened his eyes he knew for the first time that it was Minnetaki who sat close beside him, and that it was her hand that was gently stroking his forehead. From that day on he gained strength rapidly, but it was a month before he could sit up, and another two weeks before he could stand. And so it happened that it was full two months after he had made his assertion in the old cabin before Rod was in good health again.

One day Minnetaki had a tremendous surprise in store for him. Rod had never seen her look quite so pretty, or quite so timid, as she did on this particular morning.

"Will you forgive me for—for—keeping something from you, Rod?" she asked. She did not wait for the boy's reply, but went on. "When you were so sick, and we thought you might die, I wrote to your mother and we sent the letter down by a special sledge. And—and—oh, Rod, I just can't keep it in any longer, no matter if you do scold me! Your mother has come—and she is at Wabinosh House now!"

For a moment Rod stood like one struck dumb. Then he found his voice in a series of war-whoops which quickly brought Wabi in, only to see his friend dancing around Minnetaki like one gone crazy.

"Forgive you!" he shouted again and again. "Minnetaki, you're a brick—you certainly are a brick!"

As soon as Wabi was made acquainted with the cause of Roderick's excitement he also joined in the other's wild rejoicing, and their antics startled half the house of Kenegami. Mukoki shared their joy, and Wabi hugged and kissed his sister until her pretty face was like a wild rose.

"Hurrah!" shouted Wabi for the twentieth time. "That means we start on our hunt for the lost gold-mine within a fortnight!"

"It means—" began Roderick.

"It means—" interrupted Minnetaki, "it means that you're all happy but me—and I'm glad for Rod's sake, and I want to know his mother. But you're all going—and I'm to be left behind!"

There was no laughter in her voice, and Rod and Wabigoon became suddenly quiet as she turned away.

"I'm sorry," said Wabi. "But—we can't help it."

Mukoki broke the tension.

"How bright the sun shine!" he exclaimed. "Snow an' ice go. Spring—heem here!"

CHAPTER VII

ON THE TRAIL OF GOLD

And each day thereafter the sun rose earlier, and the day was longer, and the air was warmer; and with the warmth there now came the sweet scents of the budding earth and the myriad sounds of the deep, unseen life of the forests, awakening from its long slumber in its bed of snow. The moose-birds chirped their mating songs and flirted from morning till night in bough and air, and the jays and ravens fluffed themselves in the sun, and the snowbirds, little black and white beauties that were wont to whisk about like so many flashing gems, became fewer and fewer, until they were gone altogether. The poplar buds swelled more and more in their joy, until they split like over-fat peas, and the partridges feasted upon them.

And Mother Bear came out of her winter den, accompanied by her little ones born two months before, and taught them how to pull down the slender saplings for these same buds; and the moose came down from the blizzardy tops of the great ridges, which are called mountains in the North, and where for good reasons they had passed the winter, followed by the wolves, who fed upon their weak and sick. Everywhere there were the rushing torrents of melting snows, the crackle of crumbling ice, the dying frost-cries of rock and earth and tree, and each night the cold, pale glow of the Aurora Borealis crept farther and farther toward the Pole in fading glory.

It was spring, and at Wabinosh House it brought more joy than elsewhere, for there Roderick Drew joined his mother. We have not time here to dwell on the things that happened at the old Hudson Bay Post during the ten days after their first happy reunion—of the love that sprang up between Rod's mother and Minnetaki, and the princess wife of George Newsome, the factor; of the departure of the soldiers whose task of running down Woonga ended with Rod's desperate fight in the cabin, or of the preparations of the gold hunters themselves.

On a certain evening in April, Wabi, Mukoki and Rod had assembled in the latter's room. The next morning they were to start on their long and thrilling adventure into the far North, and on this last night they went carefully over their equipment and plans to see that nothing had been forgotten. That night Rod slept little. For the second time in his life the fever of adventure was running wild in his blood. After the others had gone he studied the precious old map until his eyes grew dim; in the half slumber that came to him afterward his brain worked ceaselessly, and he saw visions of the romantic old cabin again, and the rotting buckskin bag filled with nuggets of gold on the table.

He was up before the stars began fading in the dawn, and in the big dining-room of the Post, in which had gathered the factors and their families for two hundred years, the boys ate their last breakfast with those whom they were about to leave for many weeks, perhaps months. The factor himself was boisterously cheerful in his efforts to keep up the good cheer of Mrs. Drew and the princess mother, and even Minnetaki forced herself to smile, and laugh, though her eyes were red, and all knew that she had been crying. Rod was glad when the meal was over and they went out into the chill air of the morning, and down to the edge of the lake, where their big birch-bark canoe was loaded and waiting for their departure, and he was still more relieved when they had bade a last good-by to the two mothers. But Minnetaki came down to the canoe with them, and when Wabi kissed her she burst into tears, and Rod felt a queer thickening in his throat as he took her firm little hand and held it for a moment between both his own.

"Good-by, Minnetaki," he whispered.

He turned and took his position in the middle of the canoe, and with a last shout Wabi shoved off and the canoe sped out into the gloom.

For a long time there was silence, except for the rhythmic dip of the three paddles. Once Minnetaki's voice came to them faintly, and they answered it with a shout. But that was all. After a time Rod said,

"By George, this saying good-by is the toughest part of the whole business!"

His words cleared away the feeling of oppression that seemed to have fallen on them.

"It's always hard for me to leave Minnetaki," replied Wabigoon. "Some day I'm going to take her on a trip with me."

"She'd be a bully fellow!" cried Rod with enthusiasm.

From the stern of the canoe came a delighted chuckle from Mukoki.

"She brave—she shoot, she hunt, she be dam' fine!" he added, and both Rod and Wabi burst out laughing. The young Indian looked at his compass by the light of a match.

"We'll strike straight across Lake Nipigon instead of following the shore. What do you say, Muky?" he called back.

The old pathfinder was silent. In surprise Wabi ceased paddling, and repeated his question.

"Don't you think it is safe?"

Mukoki wet his hand over the side and held it above his head.

"Wind in south," he said. "Maybe no get stronger, but—"

"If she did," added Rod dubiously, noting how heavily laden the canoe was, "we'd be in a fix, as sure as you live!"

"It will take us all of to-day and half of to-morrow to follow the shore," urged Wabi, "while by cutting straight across the lake we can make the other side early this afternoon. Let's risk it!"

Mukoki grunted something that was a little less than approval, and Rod felt a peculiar sensation shoot through him as the frail birch headed out into the big lake. Their steady strokes sent the canoe through the water at fully four miles an hour, and by the time broad day had come the forest-clad shore at Wabinosh House was only a hazy outline in the distance. The white youth's unspoken fears were dispelled when the sun rose, warm and glorious, over the shimmering lake, driving the chill from the air, and seeming to bring with it the sweet scents of the forests far away. Joyfully he labored at his paddle, the mere exhilaration of the morning filling his arms with the strength of a young giant. Wabi whistled and sang wild snatches of Indian song by turns, Rod joined him with *Yankee Doodle* and *The Star Spangled Banner*, and even the silent Mukoki gave a whoop now and then to show that he was as happy as they.

One thought filled the minds of all. They were fairly started on that most thrilling of all trails, the trail of gold. In their possession was the secret of a great fortune. Romance, adventure, discovery, awaited them. The big, silent North, mysterious in its age-old desolation, where even the winds seemed to whisper of strange things that had happened countless years before, was just ahead of them. They were about to bury themselves in its secrets, to wrest from it the yellow treasure it guarded, and their blood tingled and leaped excitedly at the thought. What would be revealed to them? What might they not discover? What strange adventures were they destined to encounter in that Unknown World, peopled only by the things of the wild, that stretched trackless and unexplored before them? A hundred thoughts like these fired the brains of the three adventurers, and made their work a play, and every breath they drew one of joy.

The lake was alive with ducks. Huge flocks of big black ducks, mallards, blue bills and whistlers rose about them, and now and then, when an unusually large flock was seen floating upon the water ahead of them, one of the three would take a pot-shot with his rifle. Rod and Mukoki had each killed two, and Wabi three, when the old warrior stopped the fun.

"No waste too much shooting on ducks," he advised. "Need shells—big game."

Several times during the morning the three rested from their exertions, and at noon they ceased paddling for more than an hour while they ate the generous dinner that had been put up for them at Wabinosh House. The farther side of the lake was now plainly visible, and when the journey was resumed all eyes eagerly sought for signs of the mouth of the Ombabika, where their stirring adventures of the winter before had begun. For some time Wabi's gaze had been fixed upon a long, white rim along the shore, to which he now called his companions' attention.

"It seems to be moving," he said, turning to Mukoki. "Is it possible—" He paused doubtfully.

"What?" questioned Rod.

"That it's swans!" he completed.

"Swans!" cried the young hunter. "Great Scott, do you mean to say there could be enough swans—"

"They sometimes cover the lake in thousands," said Wabi. "I have seen them whitening the water as far as one could see."

"More swan as you count in twent' t'ous'nd year!" affirmed Mukoki. After a few moments he added, "Them no swan. Ice!"

There was an unpleasant ring in his voice as he spoke the last word, and though Rod did not fully understand what significance the discovery held for them he could not but observe that it occasioned both of his comrades considerable anxiety. The cause was not long in doubt. Another half hour of brisk paddling brought them to the edge of a frozen field of ice that extended for a quarter of a mile from the shore. In both directions it stretched beyond their vision. Wabi's face was filled with dismay. Mukoki sat with his paddle across his knees, uttering not a sound.

"What's the matter?" asked Rod. "Can't we make it?"

"Make it!" exclaimed Wabigoon. "Yes—perhaps to-morrow, or the next day!"

"Do you mean to say we can't get over that ice?"

"That's just exactly the predicament we are in. The edge of that ice is rotten."

The canoe had drifted alongside the ice, and Rod began pounding it with his paddle. For a distance of two feet it broke off in chunks, then became more firm.

"I believe that if we cut our way in for a canoe length or so it would hold us," he declared.

Wabi reached for an ax.

"We'll try it!"

Mukoki shook his head.

But for a second time that day Wabigoon persisted in acting against the old pathfinder's judgment, something that Rod had never known him to be guilty of before. Foot by foot he broke the ice ahead of the canoe, until the frail craft had thrust its length into the rotten field. Then, steadying himself on the bow, he stepped out cautiously upon the ice.

"There!" he cried triumphantly. "You next, Rod! Steady!"

In a moment Rod had joined him. What happened after that seemed to pass like a terrible nightmare. First there came a light cracking in the ice under their feet, but it was over in an instant. Wabi was laughing at him for the fear that had come into his face, and calling his name, when with a thunderous, crash the whole mass gave way under them, and they plunged down into the black depths of the lake. The last that Rod saw was his friend's horror-stricken face sinking in the crumbling ice; he heard a sharp, terrible cry from Mukoki, and then he knew that the cold waters had engulfed him, and that he was battling for his life under the surface.

Fiercely he struck out with arms and legs in an effort to rise, and in that moment of terror he thought of the great sheet of ice. What if he should come up under it? In which direction should he strike out? He opened his eyes but all was a black chaos about him.

The seconds seemed like ages. There came a splitting, rending sensation in his head, an almost overpowering desire to open his mouth, to gasp, gasp for air where there was nothing but death! Then his head struck something. It was the ice! He had come up under the ice, and there was but one end to that!

He began to sink again, slowly, as if an invisible hand were pulling him down, and in his despair he made a last frantic effort, striking out blindly, knowing that in another second he must open his mouth. Even under the water he still had consciousness enough left to know that he tried to cry out, and he felt the first gurgling rush of water into his lungs. But he did not see the long arm that reached down where the bubbles were coming up, he did not feel the grip that dragged him out upon the ice. His first sense of life was that something very heavy was upon his stomach, and that he was being rubbed, and pummeled, and rolled about as if he had become the plaything of a great bear. Then he saw Mukoki, and then Wabigoon.

"You go build fire," he heard Mukoki say, and he could hear Wabi running swiftly shoreward. For he knew that they were still upon the ice. The canoe was drawn safely up a dozen feet away, and the old Indian was dragging blankets from it. When Mukoki turned he found Rod resting upon his elbow, looking at him.

"That—w'at you call heem—close shave!" he grinned, placing a supporting arm under Rod's shoulder.

With Mukoki's assistance the youth rose to his feet, and a thick blanket was wrapped about him. Slowly they made their way shoreward, and soon Wabi came running out to meet them, dripping wet.

"Rod, when we get thawed out, I want you to kick me," he pleaded. "I want you to kick me good and hard, and then I'll take great pleasure in kicking you. And ever after this, when we do a thing that Mukoki tells us not to do, we'll kick some more!"

"Who pulled us out?" asked Rod.

"Mukoki, of course. Will you kick me?"

"Shake!"

And the two dripping, half-frozen young adventurers shook hands, while Mukoki chuckled and grunted and gurgled until he set the others bursting into laughter.

CHAPTER VIII

THE YELLOW BULLET

Before a rousing fire of logs Rod and Wabigoon began to see the cheerful side of life again, and as soon as Mukoki had built them a balsam shelter they stripped off their clothes and wrapped themselves in blankets, while the old Indian dried their outfits. It was two hours before they were dressed. No sooner were they out than Wabi went into the bush and returned a few minutes later brandishing a good-sized birch in his hand. There was no sign of humor in his face as he eyed Rod.

"Do you see that log?" he said, pointing to the big trunk of a fallen tree near the fire "That will just fit your stomach, Rod. It will be better than kicking. Double yourself over that, face down, pantaloons up. I'm going to lick you first because I want you to know just how much to give me. I want it twice as hard, for I was more to blame than you."

In some astonishment Rod doubled himself over the log.

"Great Scott!" he ejaculated, peering up in dismay. "Not too hard, Wabi!"

Swish! fell the birch, and a yell of pain burst from the white youth's lips.

Swish!—Swish!—Swish!

"Ouch! Great Caesar—Let up!"

"Don't move!" shouted Wabi. "Take it like a man—you deserve it!"

Again and again the birch fell. Rod groaned as he rose to his feet after Wabi had stopped. "Oh, please—please give me that whip!"

"Not too hard, you know," warned Wabi, as he fitted himself over the log.

"You chose your own poison," reminded Rod, rolling up his sleeve. "Just twice as hard, no more!"

And the birch began to fall.

When it was over Rod's arm ached, and Wabi, despite his Indian stoicism, let out a long howl at the last blow.

During the entire scene of chastisement Mukoki stood like one struck dumb.

"We'll never be bad any more, Muky," promised Wabigoon, rubbing himself gently. "That is, if we are, we'll whip ourselves again, eh, Rod?"

"Not so long as I can run!" assured Rod with emphasis. "I'm willing to lend a helping hand at any time you think you deserve another, but beyond that please count me out!"

For an hour after the self-punishment of the young gold hunters the three gathered fuel for the night and balsam boughs for their beds. It was dark by the time they sat down to their supper, which they ate in the light of a huge fire of dry poplar.

"This is better than paddling all night, even if we did have a close shave," said Rod, after they had finished and settled themselves comfortably.

Wabi gave a grimace and shrugged his shoulders.

"Do you know how close your call was?" he asked. "It was so close that just by one chance in ten thousand you were saved. I had pulled myself upon the ice by catching hold of the bow of the canoe and when Muky saw that I was safe he watched for you. But you didn't show up. We had given you up for dead when a few bubbles came to the surface, and quicker than a wink Mukoki thrust down his arm. He got you by the hair as you were sinking for the last time. Think of that, Rod, and dream of it to-night. It'll do you good."

"Ugh!" shuddered the white youth. "Let's talk of something more cheerful. What a glorious fire that poplar makes!"

"Mak' light more as twent' t'ous'nd candles!" agreed Mukoki. "Heem bright!"

"Once upon a time, many ages ago, there was a great chief in this country," began Wabigoon, "and he had seven beautiful daughters. So beautiful were they that the Great Spirit himself fell in love with them, and for the first time in countless moons he appeared upon earth, and told the chief that if he would give him his seven daughters he, in turn, would grant the father seven great desires. And the chief, surrendering his daughters, asked that he might be given a day without night, and a night without day, and his wish was granted; and his third and fourth and fifth desires were that the land might always be filled with fish and game, the forests remain for ever green, and fire be given to his people. His sixth desire was that a fuel be given to him which would burn even in water, and the Great Spirit gave him birch; and his seventh desire was that he might possess another fuel, which would throw off no smoke, and might bring comfort and joy to his wigwams—and the poplar sprang up in the forests. And because of that chief, and his seven beautiful daughters, all of these things are true even to this day. Isn't it so, Mukoki?"

The old warrior nodded.

"And what became of the Great Spirit and the seven beautiful daughters?" questioned Rod.

Mukoki rose and left the fire.

"He believes in that as he believes in the sun and the moon," spoke Wabi softly. "But he knows that you do not, and that all white people laugh at it. He could tell you many wonderful stories of the creation of these forests and mountains and the things in them if he would. But he knows that you would not believe, and would laugh at him afterward."

In an instant Rod was upon his feet.

"Mukoki!" he called. "Mukoki!"

The old Indian turned and came back slowly. The white youth met him half-way, his face flushed, his eyes shining.

"Mukoki," he said gently, gripping the warrior's hand, "Mukoki—I love your Great Spirit! I love the one who made these glorious forests, and that glorious moon up there, and the mountains and lakes and rivers! I Want to know more about him. You must tell me, so that I will know when he talks about me, in the winds, in the stars, in the forests! Will you?"

Mukoki was looking at him, his thin lips parted, his grim visage relaxed, as if he were weighing the truthfulness of the white youth's words.

"And I will tell you about our Great Spirit, the white man's Great Spirit," urged Rod. "For we have a Great Spirit, too, Mukoki, and He did for the white man's world what yours did for you. He created the earth, the sky and the sea and all the things in them in six days, and on the seventh He rested. And that seventh day we call Sunday, Mukoki. And He made our forests for us, as your Great Spirit made them for you, only instead of giving them for the love of seven beautiful women He gave them for the love of man. I'll tell you wonderful things about Him, Mukoki, if you will tell me about yours. Is it a bargain?"

"Mebby—yes," replied the old pathfinder slowly. His face had softened, and for the second time Rod knew that he had touched the heartstrings of his red comrade. They returned to the fire, and Wabi made room for them upon the log beside him. In his hand he held a copy of the old birch-bark map.

"I've been thinking about this all day," he said, spreading it out so that the others could see. "Somehow I haven't been able to get the idea out of my head that—"

"What?" asked Rod.

"Oh, nothing," hastily added Wabi, as if he regretted what he had said. "It's a mighty curious map, isn't it? I wonder if we'll ever know its whole story."

"I believe we know it now," declared Rod. "In the first place, we found it clutched by one of the skeletons, and we know from the knife wounds in those skeletons, and the weapons near them, that the two men fought and killed themselves. They fought for this map, for the precious secret which each wished to possess alone. Now—"

He took the map from Wabi's fingers and held it up between them and the fire.

"Isn't the rest of it clear?"

For a few moments the three looked at it in silence.

From the faded outlines of the original it had been drawn with painstaking accuracy.

With a splinter Rod pointed to the top of the map, where were written the words, "Cabin and head of chasm."

"Could anything be clearer?" he repeated. "Here is the cabin in which the men killed themselves, and where we found their skeletons, and here they have marked the chasm in which I shot the silver fox, and down which we must go to find the gold. According to this we must go until we come to the third waterfall, and there we will find another cabin—and the gold."

"It all seems very simple—by the map," agreed Wabi.

Under the crude diagram were a number of lines in writing. They were:

"We, John Ball, Henri Langlois, and Peter Plante, having discovered gold at this fall, do hereby agree to joint partnership in the same, and do pledge ourselves to forget our past differences and work in mutual good will and honesty, so help us God. Signed,

"JOHN BALL, HENRI LANGLOIS, PETER PLANTE."

Through the name of John Ball had been drawn a broad black line which had almost destroyed the letters, and at the end of this line, in brackets, was printed a word in French, which for the hundredth time Wabi translated aloud:

"Dead!"

"From the handwriting of the original we know that Ball was a man of some education," continued Rod. "And there is no doubt but that the birch-bark sketch was made by him. All of the writing was in one hand, with the exception of the signatures of Langlois and Plante, and you could hardly decipher the letters in those signatures if you did not already know their names. From these lines it is quite certain that we were right at the cabin when we concluded that the two Frenchmen killed the Englishman to get him out of the partnership. Isn't that story clear enough?"

"Yes, as far as you have gone," replied Wabi. "These three men discovered gold, quarreled, signed this agreement, and then Ball was murdered. The two Frenchmen, as Mukoki suggested at the cabin, came out a little later for supplies, and brought the buckskin bag full of gold with them. They had come as far as the cabin at the head of the chasm when they quarreled over possession of the map and agreement, fought, and died. From the old guns and other evidences we found near them we know that all this happened at least fifty years ago, and perhaps more. But—"

He paused, whistling softly.

"Where is the third waterfall?"

"I thought we settled that last winter," replied Rod, a little irritated by his companion's doubt. "If writing goes for anything, Ball was a man of education, and he drew the map according to some sort of scale. The second fall is only half as far from the first fall as the third fall is from the second, which is conclusive evidence of this. Now Mukoki discovered the first waterfall fifty miles down the chasm!"

"And we figured from the distances between John Ball's marks on the birch, that the third fall was about two hundred and fifty miles from our old camp at the head of the chasm," rejoined Wabigoon. "It looks reasonable."

"It is reasonable," declared Rod, his face flushed with excitement. "From the head of the chasm our trail is as plain as day. We can't miss it!"

Mukoki had been listening in silence, and now joined in the conversation for the first time.

"Must get to chasm first," he grunted, giving his shoulders a hunch that suggested a great deal.

Wabi returned the map to his pocket.

"You're right, Muky," he laughed. "We're climbing mountains before we come to them. It will be tough work getting to the chasm."

"Much water—ver' swift. River run lak twent' t'ous'nd cari-boo!"

"I'll bet the Ombabika is a raging torrent," said Rod.

"And we've got forty miles of it, all upstream," replied Wabi. "Then we come to the Height of Land. After that the streams run northward, to Hudson Bay, and when we reach them we'll hold our breath and pray instead of paddling. Oh, it will be exciting fun rushing down-stream on the floods!"

"But there is work before us to-morrow—hard work," said Rod. "And I'm going to bed. Good night!"

Mukoki and Wabigoon soon followed their companion's example, and half an hour later nothing but the crackling of the fire disturbed the stillness of the camp. Mukoki was as regular as clockwork in his rising, and an hour before dawn he was up and preparing breakfast. When his young comrades aroused themselves they found the ducks they had shot the preceding day roasting on spits over the fire, and coffee nearly ready. Rod also noticed that a part of the contents of the canoe were missing.

"Took load up to river," explained Mukoki in response to the youth's questioning.

"Working while we sleep, as usual," exclaimed the disgusted Wabigoon.
"If it keeps on we'll deserve another whipping, Rod!"

Mukoki examined a fat bluebill, roasted to a rich brown, and gave it to Rod. Another he handed to Wabigoon, and with a third in his own hands he found a seat for himself upon the ground close to the coffee and bread.

"Ah, if this isn't fit for a king!" cried Rod, poising his savory bluebill on the end of a fork.

Half an hour later the three went to their canoe. Mukoki had already packed a half of its contents to the river, a quarter of a mile away, and he now loaded himself with the remainder while the two boys hoisted the light birch upon their shoulders. As Roderick caught his first glimpse of the Ombabika in the growing light of day he gave a cry of astonishment. When he had gone up the stream the preceding winter it was scarce more than a dozen gun lengths in width. Now it was a veritable Amazon, its black, ugly waters rolling and twisting like the slow boiling of a thick liquid over a fire. There was little rush about it, no frenzied haste, no mountain-like madness in the advance of the torrent. Rod had expected to see this, and he would not have been startled by it.

But there was something vastly more appalling in the flood that rolled slowly before his eyes, with its lazily twisting whirlpools, its thousand unseen currents, rolling the water here and there—always in different places—like the gurgling eruptions he had often observed in a pot of simmering oatmeal. There was something uncanny about it, something terribly suggestive of giant hands under the surface, waiting to pull them down. He knew, without questioning, that there was more deadly power in that creeping flood than in a dozen boisterous torrents thundering down from the mountains. In it were the cumulative waters of a score of those torrents, and in its broad, deep sweep into the big lake the currents and perils of each were combined into one great threatening force.

The thoughts that were in Rod's mind betrayed themselves as he looked at his companions. Mukoki was reloading the canoe. Wabi watched the flood.

"She's running pretty strong," said the Indian youth dubiously. "What do you think of it, Muky?"

"Keep close to shore," replied the old warrior, without stopping his work. "We mak' heem—safe!"

There was a good deal of consolation in Mukoki's words, for both youths still bore smarting reminders of his caution and good judgment. In a short time the canoe was safely launched where a small eddy had worked into the shore, and the three adventurers dug in their paddles. Mukoki, who held the important position in the stern, kept the bow of the birch within half a dozen yards of the bank, and to Rod's mind they slipped up-stream with amazing speed and ease. Now and then one of the upheavings of the currents would catch the canoe, and from the way in which it was pitched either to one side or the other Rod easily imagined what perils the middle of the stream would have held for them. Quick action on the part of Mukoki and Wabigoon was always necessary to counteract the effect of these upheavals, and in the bow Wabi was constantly on the alert. At no time could they tell when to expect the attacks of the unseen forces below. Ten feet ahead the water might be running as smooth as oil, then—a single huge bubble, as if a great fish had sent up a gasp of air—and in an instant it would be boiling like a small maelstrom.

Rod noticed that each time they were caught near one of these some unseen power seemed sucking them down, and that at those times the canoe would settle several inches deeper than when they were in calm water. The discovery thrilled him, and he wondered what one of the big eruptions out in mid-stream would do to them if they were caught in it. Other perils were constantly near them. Floating logs and masses of brush and other debris swept down with the flood, and Wabi's warning cries of "right," "left," and "back" came with such frequency that Rod's arms ached with the mighty efforts which he made with his paddle in response to them. Again the stream would boil with such fury ahead of them that Mukoki would put in to shore, and a portage would be made beyond the danger point. Five times during the day were the canoe and its contents carried in this manner, so that including all time lost an average of not more than two miles an hour was made. When camp was struck late that afternoon, however, Mukoki figured that they had covered half the distance up the Ombabika.

The following day's progress was even slower. With every mile the stream became narrower and swifter. The treacherous upheavals caused by undercurrents no longer harassed the gold seekers, but logs and debris swept down with greater velocity. Several times the frail canoe was saved from destruction only by the quick and united action of the three. They worked now like a well-regulated machine, engineered by Wabigoon, whose sharp eyes were always on the alert for danger ahead. This second day was one of thrills and tense anxiety for Rod, and he was glad when it came to an end. It was early, and the sun was still two hours high, when they stopped to camp.

Mukoki had chosen an open space, backed by a poplar-covered rocky ridge, and scarce had the bow of the canoe touched shore when Wabi gave an excited exclamation, caught up his rifle, and fired three rapid shots in the direction of a small clump of spruce near the foot of the mountain.

"Missed, by all that's good and great!" he yelled. "Quick, Mukoki, shove her in! There's the biggest bear I've seen in all my life!"

"Where?" demanded Rod. "Where is he?"

He dropped his paddle and snatched his own rifle, while Mukoki, keeping his self-possession, brought the canoe so that Wabi could leap ashore. Rod followed like a flash, and the two excited youths sped in the direction of the bear, leaving their companion to care for himself and the heavily-laden birch. A short, swift run brought them to the edge of the spruce, and with hearts beating wildly the two scanned the barren side of the mountain ahead of them. There was no sign of the bear.

"He turned down-stream!" cried Wabi, "We must cut—"

"There he is," whispered Rod sharply.

Just beginning the ascent of the mountain, four or five hundred yards below them, was the bear. Even at that distance Rod was amazed at the size of the beast.

"What a monster!" he gasped.

"Blaze away!" urged Wabi. "It's four hundred yards if it's a foot! Aim for the top of his back and you'll bring him!"

Suiting action to his words he fired the two remaining shots in his rifle, and as he slipped in fresh cartridges Rod continued the long-range fusillade. His first and second shots produced no effect. At his third the running animal paused for a moment and looked down at them, and the young Hunter seized his opportunity to take a careful aim. At the report of his gun the bear gave a quick lunge forward, half-fell among the rocks, and then was off again.

"You hit him!" shouted Wabi, setting off on a dead run between the spruce and the mountain.

For a few brief moments Rod studied the situation as he reloaded. The bear was rapidly nearing the summit of the ridge. By, swift running Wabigoon would have another fair shot before the animal got out of range. If that shot were a miss they would lose their game. In a flash he discerned a break in the mountain. If he could make that, and the bear turned in his direction—

Without further thought he ran toward the break. He heard the sharp reports of Wabi's rifle behind him, but didn't stop to see the effect of the fire. If it was another miss— every second counted. The cut in the mountain was clear. Breathlessly he dashed through it and stopped on the opposite side, his eyes eagerly scanning the rock-strewn ridge. He made no attempt to suppress the exclamation of joy that came to his lips when, fully eight hundred yards away, he discerned the bear coming down the side of the mountain, and in his direction. Crouching behind a huge boulder Rod waited. Seven hundred yards, six hundred, five hundred, and the bear turned, this time striking into the edge of the plain. The animal was traveling slowly, partly stopping in his flight now and then, and Rod knew that he was badly wounded. It was soon evident that the course being taken by the game would bring it no nearer, and the young hunter leveled his rifle.

Five hundred yards, more than a quarter of a mile!

This was desperate shooting, shooting that sent a strange thrill through Roderick Drew. The magnificent weapon in his hands was equal to the task. It would kill easily at that distance. But would he fail? He was confident that his first shot went high. His second had no effect. To his third there came the sharp response of a fourth from the top of the mountain. Wabigoon had reached the summit, and was firing at six hundred yards!

The bear stopped. With deadly precision Rod now took aim at the motionless animal. An instant after he had fired a wild shout burst from his throat, and was answered by Wabigoon's joyful yell from the mountain. It was a wonderful shot, and the bear was down!

The animal was dead when the triumphant young hunters reached its side. It was some time before either of them spoke. Panting from their exertions, both looked down in silence upon the huge beast at their feet. That he had made a remarkable kill Rod could see by the look of wonder in his companion's face. They were still mutely regarding the dead animal when Mukoki came through the break in the ridge and hurried toward them. His face, too, became filled with amazement when he saw the bear.

"Big bear!" he exclaimed.

There was a world of meaning in his words, and Rod flushed with pleasure.

"He weighs five hundred," said Wabi, "and he stands four feet at the shoulders if an inch."

"Fine rug!" grinned Mukoki.

"Let's see, Rod; he'll make a rug—" Wabi walked critically around the bear. "He'll make you a rug over eight feet long by about six in width. I wonder where he is hit?"

A brief examination showed that while the honors of the actual kill were with Rod, at least one, and perhaps two, of Wabi's shots had taken effect. The last shot from the white youth's rifle had struck the bear just below the right ear, causing almost instantaneous death. On this same side, which had been exposed to Rod's fire, was a body wound, undoubtedly made by the shot on the mountain side. When the animal was rolled over by the combined efforts of the three two more wounds were discovered on the left side, which had mostly been exposed to Wabigoon's fire. It was while examining these that the sharp-eyed Mukoki gave a sudden grunt of surprise.

"Heem shot before—long time ago! Old wound—feel bullet!"

Between his fingers he was working the loose hide back of the foreleg. The scar of an old wound was plainly visible, and both Rod and Wabi could feel the ball under the skin. There is something that fascinates the big game hunter in this discovery of an old wound in his quarry, and especially in the vast solitudes of the North, where hunters are few and widely scattered. It brings with it a vivid picture of what happened long ago, the excitement of some other chase, the well-directed shot, and at last the escape of the game. And so it was now. The heads of Rod and Wabigoon hung close over Mukoki's shoulders while the old Indian dug out the bullet with his knife. Another grunt of surprise fell from the pathfinder's lips as he dropped the pellet in the palm of his hand.

It was a strange-looking object, smooth, and curiously flattened.

"Ver' soft bullet," said Mukoki. "Never know lead thin, thin out lak that!"

With his knife he peeled off a thin slice of the ball.

"Heem—"

He held up the two pieces. In the sun they gleamed a dull, rich yellow.

"That bullet made of gold!" he breathed, scarcely above a whisper. "No yellow lead. That gold, pure gold!"

CHAPTER IX

UP THE OMBABIKA

For a few moments after Mukoki's remarkable discovery the three stood speechless. Wabigoon stared as if he could not bring himself to believe the evidence of his eyes. Rod was quivering with the old, thrilling excitement that had first come to him in the cabin where they had found the skeletons and the buckskin bag with its precious nuggets, and Mukoki's face was a study. The thin, long fingers which held the two pieces of the gold bullet trembled, which was an unusual symptom in the old pathfinder. It was he who broke the silence, and his words gave utterance to the question which had rushed into the heads of the two young hunters.

"Who shoot gold bullets at bear?"

And to this question there was, for the time, absolutely no answer. To tell who shot that bullet was impossible. But why was it used?

Wabigoon had taken the parts of the yellow ball and was weighing them in the palm of his hand.

"It weighs an ounce," he declared.

"Twenty dollars' worth of gold!" gasped Rod, as if he lacked breath to express himself. "Who in the wide world is shooting twenty dollar bullets at bear?" he cried more excitedly, repeating Mukoki's question of a minute before.

He, too, weighed the yellow pellets in his hand.

The puzzled look had gone out of Mukoki's face. 'Again the battle-scarred old warrior wore the stoic mask of his race, which only now and then is lifted for an instant by some sudden and unexpected happening. Behind that face, immobile, almost expressionless, worked a mind alive to every trick and secret of the vast solitudes, and even before his young comrades had gained the use of their tongues he was, in his savage imagination, traveling swiftly back over the trail of the monster bear to the gun that had fired the golden bullet. Wabigoon understood him, and watched him eagerly.

"What do you think of it, Muky?"

"Man shoot powder and ball gun, not cartridge," replied Mukoki slowly. "Old gun. Strange; ver' strange!"

"A muzzle loader!" said Wabi.

The Indian nodded.

"Had powder, no lead. Got hungry; used gold."

Eight words had told the story, or at least enough of it to clear away a part of the cloud of mystery, but the other part still remained.

Who had fired the bullet, *and where had the gold come from?*

"He must have struck it rich," said Wabi "else would he have a chunk of gold like that?"

"Where that come from—more, much! more," agreed Mukoki shortly.

"Do you suppose—" began Rod. There was a curious thrill in his voice, and he paused, as if scarce daring to venture the rest of what he had meant to say. "Do you suppose— somebody has found—our gold?"

Mukoki and Wabigoon stared at him as if he had suddenly exploded a mine. Then Wabi turned and looked silently at the old Indian. Not a word was spoken. Silently Rod drew something from his pocket, carefully wrapped in a bit of cloth.

"You remember I kept this little nugget from my share in the buckskin bag, intending to have a scarf-pin made of it," he explained. "When I took my course in geology and mineralogy I learned that, if one had half a dozen specimens of gold, each from a different mine, the chances were about ten to one that no two of them would be exactly alike in coloring. Now—"

He exposed the nugget, and made a fresh cut in it with his knife, as Mukoki had done with the yellow bullet. Then the two gleaming surfaces were compared.

One glance was sufficient.

The gold was the same!

Wabi drew back, uttering something under his breath, his eyes gleaming darkly. Rod's face had suddenly turned a shade whiter, and Mukoki, not understanding the mysteries of mineralogy, stared at the youth in mute suspense.

"Somebody has found our gold!" cried Wabi, almost savagely.

"We are not sure," interrupted Rod. "We know only that the evidence is very suspicious. The rock formation throughout this country is almost identically the same, deep trap on top, with slate beneath, and for that reason it is very possible that gold found right in this locality would be of exactly the same appearance as gold found two hundred miles from here. Only—it's suspicious," Rod concluded.

"Man probably dead," consoled Mukoki. "No lead—hungry—shoot bear an' no git heem. Mebby starve!"

"The poor devil!" exclaimed Wabigoon. "We've been too selfish to give a thought to that, Rod. Of course he was hungry, or he wouldn't have used gold for bullets. And he didn't get this bear! By George—"

"I wish he'd got him," said Rod simply.

Somehow Mukoki's words sent a flush into his face. There came to him, suddenly, a mental picture of that possible tragedy in the wilderness: the starving man, his last hopeless molding of a golden bullet, the sight of the monster bear, the shot, and after that the despair and suffering and slow death of the man who had fired it.

"I wish he'd got it," he repeated. "We have plenty of grub."

Mukoki was already at work skinning the bear, and Rod and Wabigoon unsheathed their knives and joined him.

"Wound 'bout fi', six month old," said the Indian. "Shot just before snow."

"When there wasn't a berry in the woods for a starving man to eat," added Wabi. "Well, here's hoping he found something, Rod."

An hour later the three gold seekers returned to their canoe laden with the choicest of the bear meat, and the animal's skin, which was immediately stretched between two trees, high up out of the reach of depredating animals. Rod gazed at it proudly.

"We'll be sure and get it when we come back, won't we?"

"Sure," replied Wabi.

"It will be safe?"

"As safe as though it were at home."

"Unless somebody comes along and steals it," added Rod.

Wabi was busy unloading certain necessary articles from the canoe, but he ceased his work to look at Rod.

"Steal!" he cried in astonishment.

Mukoki, too, had heard Rod's remark and was listening.

"Rod," continued Wabigoon quietly, "that is one thing we don't have up here. Our great big glorious North doesn't know the word thief, except when it is applied to a Woonga. If a white hunter came along here to-morrow, and found that hide stretched so low that the animals were getting at it, he would nail it higher for us. An Indian, if he camped here, would build his fire so that the sparks wouldn't strike it. Rod, up here, where we don't know civilization, we're honest!"

"But down in the States," said Rod, "the Indians steal."

The words slipped from him. The next instant he would have given anything to have been able to recall them. Mukoki had grown a little more tense in his attitude.

"That's because white men have lived so much among them, white men who are called civilized," answered the young scion of Wabinosh House, his eyes growing bright.

"White blood makes thieves. Pardon me for saying it, Rod, but it does, at least among Indians. But our white blood up here is different from yours. It's the same blood that's in our Indians, every drop of it honest, loyal to its friends, and it runs red and strong with the love of this great wilderness. There are exceptions, of course, as you have seen in the Woongas, who are an outlaw race. But we are honest, and Mukoki there, if he were dying of cold, wouldn't steal a skin to save himself. An ordinary Indian might take it, if he were dying for want of it, but not unless he had a gun to leave in its place!"

"I didn't mean to say what I did," said Rod. "Oh, I wish I were one of you! I love this big wilderness, and everything in it, and it's glorious to hear you say what you do!"

"You are one of us," cried Wabi, gripping his hand.

That evening, after they had finished their supper and the three were gathered about the fire, Wabigoon said:

"Muky could tell you one reason why the Indians of the North are honest if he wanted to, Rod. But he won't, so I will. There was once a tribe in the country of Mukoki's fore-fathers, along the Makoki River, which empties into the Albany, whose men were great thieves, and who stole from one another. No man's snare was safe from his neighbor, fights and killings were of almost daily occurrence, and the chief of the tribe was the greatest thief of all, and of course escaped punishment. This chief loved to set his own snares, and one day he was enraged to find that one of his tribe had been so bold as to set a snare within a few inches of his own, and in the trail of the same animal. He determined on meting out a terrible punishment, and waited.

"While he was waiting a rabbit ran into the snare of his rival. Picking up a stick he approached to kill the game, when suddenly there seemed to pass a white mist before his eyes, and when he looked again there was no rabbit, but the most wonderful creature he had ever beheld in the form of man, and he knew that it was the Great Spirit, and fell upon his face. And a great voice came to him, as if rolling from far beyond the most distant mountains, and it told him that the forests and streams of the red man's heaven were closed to him and his people, that in the hunting-grounds that came after death there was no place for thieves.

"'Go to your people,' he said, 'and tell them this. Tell them that from this day on, moon upon moon, until the end of time, must they live like brothers, setting their snares side by side without war, to escape the punishment that hovers over them.'

"And the chief told his people this," finished Wabi, "and from that hour there was no more thievery in the land. And because the Great Spirit came in the form he did the rabbit is the good luck animal of the Crees and Chippewayans of the far North, and wherever the snows fall deep, men set their traps side by side to this day, and do not rob."

Rod had listened with glowing eyes.

"It's glorious!" he repeated. "It's glorious, if it's true!"

"It is true," said Wabi. "In all this great country between here and the Barren Lands, where the musk-ox lives, there is not one Indian in a hundred who would steal another Indian's trap, or the game in it. It is one of the understood laws of the North that every hunter shall have his 'trap line,' or 'run,' and it is not courtesy for another trapper to encroach upon it; but if he should, and he should lay a trap close beside another's, it would not be wrong, for the law of the Great Spirit is greater than the law of man. Why, last winter even the outlaw Woongas made no effort to steal our traps, though they thirsted for our lives!"

"Mukoki," said Rod, rising, "I want to shake hands with you before I go to bed. I'm learning—fast. I wish I were half Indian!"

The next morning the journey up the Ombabika was resumed, and a little more of anxiety was now mingled with the enthusiasm of the adventurers. For no one of them could relieve himself of the possible significance of the gold bullet, the fear that their treasure had been discovered by another. Wabi regained his confidence first.

"I don't believe it!" he exclaimed at last. Without questioning, the others knew to what he referred. "I don't believe that our gold has been found. It is in the heart of the wildest country on the continent, and surely if such a rich find had been made we would have heard something about it at Wabinosh House or Kenegami, which are the nearest points of supply."

"Or, if it was found, the discoverer is dead," added Rod.

"Yes."

In the stern, Mukoki nodded and grunted his conviction.

"Dead," he repeated.

The Ombabika had now become narrow and violent. Against its swift current the canoe made but little headway, and at noon Mukoki announced that the river journey was at an end. For a few moments Rod did not recognize where they had landed. Then he gave a sudden cry of glad surprise.

"Why, this is where we had supper that night after our terrible adventure on the river last winter," he exclaimed.

From far off there came faintly to his ears a low, rumbling thunder.

"Listen! That's the river rushing through the break in the mountain where we walked the edge of the precipice!"

Wabi shrugged his shoulders at the memory of that fearful night and its desperate race to escape from the Woonga country.

"We've got to do the same thing again, only this time it will be in daylight."

"Long portage," said Mukoki. "Six mile. Carry everything."

"Until we reach the little creek in the plains beyond the mountain, where you shot the caribou?" asked Rod.

"Yes," replied Wabigoon. "That little creek will now be a pretty husky stream, and by hard work we can paddle up it until we come within about eight miles of our old camp at the head of the chasm, where we found the skeletons and the map."

"And from that point we shall have to carry our canoe and supplies to the creek in the chasm," finished Rod. "And then—hurrah for the gold!"

"Mak' old camp on mountain by night," said Mukoki.

Wabi broke into a happy laugh and thumped Rod on the back.

"Remember the big lynx you shot, Rod, and thought it was a Woonga, and had us all frightened out of our wits?" he cried.

Rod colored at the memory of his funny adventure, which was thrilling enough at the time, and began assisting Mukoki in unloading the canoe. Two hours were taken for dinner and rest, and then the young hunters shouldered their canoe while Mukoki hurried on ahead of them, weighted with a half of their supplies. Every step now brought the thunder of the torrent rushing through the mountain more clearly to their ears, and they had not progressed more than a mile when they were compelled to shout to make each other hear. On their right the wall of the mountain closed in rapidly, and as they stumbled with their burden over a mass of huge boulders the two boys saw just ahead of them the narrow trail at the edge of the precipice.

At its beginning they rested their canoe. On one side of them, a dozen yards away, the face of the mountain rose sheer above them for a thousand feet; on the other, scarce that distance from where they stood, was the roaring chasm. And ahead of them the mountain wall and the edge of the precipice came nearer and nearer, until there was no more than a six-foot ledge to walk upon. Rod's face turned strangely white as he realized, for the first time, the terrible chances they had taken on that black, eventful night of a few months ago; and for a time Wabi stood silent, his face as hard-set as a rock. Up out of the chasm there came a deafening thunder of raging waters, like the hollow explosions of great guns echoing and reëchoing in subterranean caverns.

"Let's take a look!" shouted Wabi close up to his companion's ear.

He went to the edge of the precipice, and Rod forced himself to follow, though there was in him a powerful inclination to hug close to the mountain wall. For half a minute he stood fascinated, terror-stricken, and yet in those thirty seconds he saw that which would remain with him for a lifetime. Five hundred feet below him the over-running floods of spring were caught between the ragged edges of the two chasm walls, beating themselves in their fury to the whiteness of milk froth, until it seemed as though the earth itself must tremble under their mad rush. Now and then through the twisting foam there shot the black crests of great rocks, as though huge monsters of some kind were at play, whipping the torrent into greater fury, and bellowing forth thunderous voices when they rose triumphant for an instant above the sweep of the flood.

All this Rod saw in less than a breath, and he drew back, shivering in every fiber of his body. But Wabigoon did not move. For several minutes the Indian youth stood looking down upon the wonderful force at play below him, his body as motionless as though hewn out of stone, the wild blood in his veins leaping in response to the tumult and thunder of the magnificent spectacle deep down in the chasm. When he turned to Rod his lips made no sound, but his eyes glowed with that half-slumbering fire which came only when the red blood of the princess mother gained ascendency, and the wild in him called out greeting to the savage in nature. It is not music, or fine talk, or artificial wonders that waken a thrill deep down in the Indian soul, it is the great mountain, the vast plain, the roaring cataract! And so it was with Wabigoon.

They went on, now, with the canoe upon their shoulders, and hugging close to the mountain wall. Slowly, avoiding every stone and stick that might cause one of them to stumble, they passed along the perilously narrow ledge, and did not rest again until they had come in safety to the broader trail leading up the mountain. An hour later Mukoki met them on his return for the remainder of their supplies. Shortly after this they reached the small plateau where they had camped during the previous winter, and lowered their canoe close to the old balsam shelter.

Everything was as they had left it. Neither snow nor storm had destroyed their lodging of boughs. There were the charred remains of their fire, the bones of the huge lynx which Roderick had thought was an attacking Woonga, and had killed; and beside the shelter was a stake driven into the ground, the stake to which they had fastened their faithful comrade of many an adventure, the tame wolf.

To this stake went Wabigoon, speaking no word. He sat down close beside it, with his arm resting upon it, and when he looked up at Rod there was an expression in his face which spoke more than words.

"Poor old Wolf!"

Rod turned and walked to the edge of the plateau, something hot and uncomfortable filling his eyes. Below him, as far as he could see, there stretched the vast, mysterious wilderness that reached to Hudson Bay. And somewhere out there in that limitless space was Wolf.

As he looked, the hot film clouding his vision, he thought of the old tragedy in Mukoki's life, and of how Wolf had helped him to avenge himself. In his imagination he went back to that terrible day many, many years ago, when Mukoki, happy in the strength of his youth, found his young wife and child dead upon the trail, killed by wolves; he thought of the story that Wabi had told him of the madness that came to the young warrior, of how year after year he followed the trail of wolves, wreaking his vengeance on their breed. And last he thought of Wolf—how Mukoki and Wabigoon had found the whelp in one of their traps; how they tamed him, grew to love him, and taught him to decoy other wolves to their riffes. Wolf had been their comrade of a few months before; fearless, faithful, until at last, escaping from the final murderous assault of the Woongas, he had fled into the forests, while his human friends fought their way back to civilization.

Where was Wolf now?

Unconsciously Rod questioned himself aloud, and from close behind him Wabi answered.

"With the hunt-pack, Rod. He's forgotten us; gone back to the wild."

"Gone back to the wild, yes," said Rod; "but forgotten us, no!"

Wabi made no reply.

CHAPTER X

THE MYSTERIOUS SHOT

For many minutes the two stood silently gazing into the North. At their feet spread the broad plain where Mukoki had killed the caribou while they watched him from the plateau; beyond that were the dense stretches of forest, broken here and there by other plains and meadows, and a dozen lakes glistened in the red tints of the setting sun. When Rod first looked upon that country a few months before it was a world of ice and snow, a cold, dazzling panorama of white that reached from where he stood to the Pole. Now it was wakening under the first magic touch of spring. Far away the two young gold hunters caught a glimmer of the stream which they were to follow up to the chasm. Last winter it had been a tiny creek; now it was swollen to the size of a river.

Suddenly, as they looked, two dark objects came slowly out into an opening a mile away. At that distance they appeared hardly larger than dogs, and Rod, whose mind was still filled with thoughts of Wolf, exclaimed "Wolves!"

In the same breath he caught himself, and added:

"Moose!"

"A cow and her calf," said Wabi.

"How do you know?" asked Rod.

"There; watch them now!" cried Wabi, catching his companion by the arm. "The mother is ahead, and even from here I can see that she is pacing. A moose never trots or gallops, like a deer, but paces, using both feet on a side at the same time. Notice how the calf jumps about. An old moose would never do that."

"But both animals look to be about the same size," replied Rod, still doubtful.

"It's a two-year-old calf; almost as big as its mother. In fact, it's not really a calf, because it is too old; but so long as young moose stick to their mothers we call them calves up here. I've known them to remain together for three years."

"They're coming this way!" whispered the white youth.

The moose had turned, heading for the base of the mountain upon which they stood. Wabi drew his companion behind a big rock, from which both could look down without being seen.

"Be quiet!" he warned. "They're coming to feed on the sprouting poplar along the mountain side. Just been over to the creek to get a drink. We may have some fun!"

He wet a finger in his mouth and held it above his head, the forest pathfinder's infallible method of telling how the wind blows. No matter how slight the movement of the air may be, one side of the finger dries first, in an instant, and is warm, while the side that remains damp is cold, and in the lee, that side toward which the wind is blowing.

"The wind is wrong, dead wrong," said Wabi. "It's blowing straight toward them. Unless we are so high that our scent goes above them they won't come much nearer."

Another minute and Rod nudged Wabigoon.

"They're within range!"

"Yes, but we won't shoot. We don't need meat."

As the young Indian spoke the cow brought herself to a dead stop so suddenly that Wabi gave a delighted grunt.

"Great!" he whispered. "She's caught a whiff of us, a quarter of a mile away. See how she holds her head, her great ears chucked forward to hear, her nose half to the sky! She knows there's danger on this mountain. Now—"

He did not finish. Like a flash the cow had darted ahead of her calf, seeming to shoulder it back, and in another moment the two were racing swiftly into the North, the mother this time in the rear instead of leading.

"I love moose," said Wabi, his eyes glowing. "Do you notice that I never shoot them, Rod?"

"By George, so you don't! I never thought of it. What is the reason?"

"There are a good many reasons. Of course I have shot them, when in very great need of meat; but it's an unpleasant job for me. You call the lion the king of beasts. Well, he isn't. The moose is monarch of them all. You saw how the mother moose acted. She led her calf when approaching, because if there should be danger she wanted to meet it first; and when she found danger she drove her calf ahead of her in retreat, so that if harm came to either of them it would come to her. Isn't that the human mother instinct? And the bull is glorious! In the mating season he will face a dozen men in defense of his cow. If she falls first he will stand between her body and the hunters' rifles, pawing the earth, his eyes glaring defiance, until he is riddled with bullets. Once I saw a wounded cow, and as she staggered away the big bull that was with her hugged her close behind, never for a moment leaving her exposed to the fire, but unflinchingly taking every bullet in his own body. So beautiful was his courage that you would not have known he was wounded until he fell dead in his tracks, literally cut to pieces. It was that sight that made me swear never to kill another moose—unless I had to."

Rod was silent. The mother and the calf had disappeared when he turned to Wabigoon.

"I'm glad you told me that, Wabi," he said. "You are teaching me new things about this big wilderness every day. I've shot one moose. I won't shoot another unless we need him."

They went back to their old camp, and by the time Mukoki returned with his second load everything was in shape for the night, and a supper of delicious bear steaks, coffee and "hot-stone biscuits," as Rod called their baked combination of flour, water and salt, was soon ready. After their meal the three sat for a long time near the fire, for there was still a slight chill in the night air, and talked mostly about Wolf and his adventures. Rod, in his distant home in civilization had read and heard much that was false about wild animals, was confident that Wolf would find they had returned into the wilderness and would join them again, and to corroborate his belief he narrated several stories of similar happenings. Wabigoon listened courteously to him, which is the way of the Indian. Then he said:

"Such stories as those are false, Rod. When I spent my year at school with you I read dozens of stories about wild animals, and very few of them were true. All sorts of people write about the wilderness, and yet not one out of a hundred of those same people have ever been in the real wilderness. And it is wonderful what some of them make wild animals do!"

Rod straightened himself with a jerk.

"I have been here only a few months, Wabi, and yet I have seen more wonderful things about animals than I have ever read in print," he declared.

"Of course you have," agreed his companion. "And there is just the point I want to make clear. Wild animals are the most wonderful creatures in existence, and if some of their actual habits and adventures were told they would be laughed at down where you came from. Where your writers make their mistake is in bringing them into too close association with human beings, and making them half human. Wolf remained with us because he knew no better. We caught him when he was a whelp, and as he grew older both Mukoki and I could see that at times he was filled with a wild longing to join his people. We knew that it was coming. He will never return to us."

Mukoki made a soft sound deep down in his throat, and Rod turned suddenly toward him.

"You believe that, Mukoki?"

"Wolf gone!"

"But animals think, don't they?" persisted Rod, to whom the discussion was of absorbing interest. "They reason, they remember!"

"They do all of that," replied Wabi, "and more. I have read certain so-called natural history stories which ridiculed the idea of wild animals possessing mental abilities, and which ascribed pretty nearly all their actions to instinct. Such stories are as wrong as those which give wild animals human endowments. Animals do think. Don't you suppose that mother moose was thinking when she stopped out there in the plain? Wasn't she turning the situation over in her mind, if you want to speak of it as that, and mentally figuring just where the danger lay, and in which direction she ought to take flight? And besides reason wild animals have instinct. One proof of this is their sixth sense; the sense of—of—what do you call it?"

"Orientation?" assisted Rod.

"Yes; that's it. Orientation. A bear, for instance, doesn't carry a compass with him, as some nature writers would like to have you believe, and yet he can go from this mountain to a den a hundred miles away as straight as a bird can fly. That's instinct."

"Then Wolf—" mused Rod slowly.

"Is with the hunt pack," finished the young Indian.

Mukoki spoke softly, as though to himself.

"Last winter the snow came, and now it is water. Two moons past, Wolf, heem tame. Now wild. The Great Spirit say that is right, I guess so."

"He means that it is nature," said Wabi.

For an hour after the others had wrapped themselves in their blankets Rod sat alone beside the fire, listening, and thinking. And after that he went to the edge of the plateau, and watched the great spring moon as it floated slowly over the vast, still wilderness. How wonderful these solitudes were, how little the teeming millions of civilization knew about them! Somehow, in those moments, as he watched the shivering Northern Lights playing far beyond the farthest footstep of man, there came to Roderick Drew the thought that God must be nearer to earth here than anywhere else in the world. For the first time his soul was filled with something that was almost love for the red man's Great Spirit. And why not? For was not that Great Spirit his own God? Sad, lonely, silent, mysterious, a whole world lay before him, a world that was the Indian Bible, that contained for the red man of the North the teachings and the voice of the Creator of all things. A wind had risen and was whispering over the plains; he heard the hushed voices of the quivering poplar boughs, and there came from far below him the soft, chuckling, mating hoot of an owl. Gradually his eyes closed, and he leaned more heavily upon the rock against which he had seated himself. After that he dreamed of what he had looked upon, while the fire at the camp died away, and Mukoki and Wabigoon slumbered, oblivious of his absence.

Of how long he slept Rod had no idea. He was suddenly brought back into wakefulness by a sound that startled him to the marrow of his bones, a terrible scream close to his ears. He sat bolt upright, quaking in every limb. For a moment he tried to cry out, but his tongue clove to the roof of his mouth. What had happened? Was it Wabi, or Mukoki?

A dozen paces away was a huge rock and as he looked he saw something move upon it, a long, lithe object that shone a silvery white in the moonlight, and he knew that it was a lynx. Stealthily Rod reached for his rifle, which had slipped between his knees, and as he did so the lynx sent forth another of its blood-curdling screams. Even now the white youth shivered at the sound, so much like the terrible cry of some person in dying agony. He leveled his gun. There was a flash in the moonlight, a sharp report, and a shout from the direction of the camp. In another moment Rod was upon his feet, and sorry that he had shot. It flashed upon him that he might have watched the lynx, one of the night pirates of all this strange wilderness, and that its pelt, at this season, would be worthless. He went to the rock cautiously. The lynx was not there. He walked around it, holding his rifle in readiness for attack. The lynx was gone. He had made a clean miss!

Both Mukoki and Wabigoon met him on the opposite side of the rock.

"'Nother heap big Woonga," grinned the old pathfinder remembering Rod's former adventure on this same plateau. "Kill?"

"Missed!" said Rod shortly. "What a scream that was! Ugh!"

This time he went to bed with the others, and slept until early dawn. The morning was one of those rare gifts of budding spring, warm and redolent with the sweetness of new life, and its beauty acted as a tonic on the three adventurers. Their fears of the day before were gone, and with song and whistle and cheery voice they began the descent of the mountain. Mukoki went on ahead of Rod and Wabigoon with his pack, and the two boys had not made more than two of the six miles in the portage across the plain when he met them again, returning for his second load. By noon the canoe and its contents were safely at the creek, and the gold hunters halted until after dinner. The little stream across which Rod had easily leaped without wetting his feet a few weeks before had swollen into a fair-sized river, and in places its searching waters had formed tiny lakes. Unlike the Ombabika, sweeping down from its mountain heights, there was but little current here, a fact that immensely pleased Mukoki and his companions.

"We near mak' cabin to-night," said the old Indian. "I take load to-night."

During the two hours' paddle up-stream Mukoki spoke but little, and as they approached nearer to their last winter's thrilling fight with the Woongas, in which they had so nearly lost their lives, he ceased even to respond by nod or grunt to the conversation of his companions. Once Wabigoon spoke again of Wolf, and for an instant the old Indian, who was in the bow, half turned to them, and for two strokes his paddle rested in mid air. From the stern Wabi reached forward and poked Rod, and the white youth understood. Next to Minnetaki and Wabigoon, and perhaps himself, he knew that the faithful pathfinder loved Wolf best, and that; he was filled with a little of that savage madness which came to him now and then when he dwelt on the terrible tragedy that had entered his life many years before. When the hunters reached the end of their canoe journey up the stream Mukoki silently shouldered his pack and set out over the plain. He spoke no word, made no sign.

"It would be useless," said Wabigoon, as Rod made a movement as if to follow and stop their comrade. "No persuasion could turn Mukoki now. He wants to reach the old camp to-night, where Wolf disappeared. He won't be back until morning."

And Mukoki went on, never for an instant turning his face, until his companions lost sight of him. But once out of their vision his, manner took on a strange and sudden change. He lowered the head strap of his pack over his breast, so that he might clutch at it with one hand, and move his head freely. His eyes glowed with the dull fire of wakening excitement; his steps were quick, and yet cautious, every movement in his advance was one of listening and watchful expectancy. A person watching the old warrior would have said that he was keenly on the alert for game, or danger. And yet the safety of his rifle was locked, a fresh trail of bear aroused no new interest in him, and when he heard a crashing in the brush on his right, where a buck had got wind of him, he gave but a single glance in its direction. He was not seeking game. Nor were his fears aroused by suspicion of possible danger. Wherever the ground was soft and moist he traveled slowly, with his eyes on the earth, and at one of these spots he came to a sudden pause. Before him were the clearly defined imprints of a wolf's feet.

With a low cry Mukoki threw off his pack and fell upon his knees. His eyes burned fiercely now. There was something of madness in the way in which he groveled in the soft earth, creeping from one footprint to the next ahead of it, and stopping always where the right forefoot had left its track. It was that foot which had held Wolf a captive in Mukoki's trap, and he had lost two toes. None was missing here, and the old pathfinder rose to his feet again, disappointment shadowing the twitching expectancy in his face.

Five times that afternoon Mukoki fell on his knees beside the trails of wolves, and five times the light of hope went out for a moment in his eyes. It was sunset when he climbed the mountain ridge to the little lake hidden away in the dip; only a last pale glow tinted the sky behind the forests when he set down his pack close to the charred remains of the old cabin. For many minutes he rested, his gaze fixed on those blackened reminders of their thrilling battle for life the winter before. His wild blood leaped again at the thought of the strife, of the desperate race that he and Roderick had run over the mountain to the burning cabin, and of their rescue of Wabigoon. Suddenly his eyes caught the white gleam of something half a hundred paces away, and he rose and walked toward it, grunting and chuckling in half-savage pleasure. The Woongas had not returned to bury their dead, and the bones beside which he stopped were those of the outlaw whom Wabigoon had killed, picked clean by the small animals of the forest.

Mukoki returned to his pack and sat down As darkness fell about him he made no effort to build a fire. He had brought food, but did not eat it. More dense grew the shadows in the forest, thicker the gloom that hung over the mountains. Still he sat, silent, listening. To him, softly and timidly at first, came the sounds of the night: the chuckling notes of birds that awakened when the earth masked itself in darkness, the hoot of an owl, the faint wailing echo of a far-away lynx cry, the plunge of a mink in the lake. And now the wind began whispering in the balsams, singing gently its age-old song of loneliness, of desolation, of mystery, and Mukoki straightened himself and looked to where the red glow of the moon was rising above the mountain. After a little he rose to his feet, took his rifle, and climbed to the summit of the ridge, with a thousand miles of wilderness sweeping between him and the Arctic sea somewhere out there in that wilderness—was Wolf!

The moon rose higher. It disclosed the old Indian, as rigid as a rock, with his back to a white, barkless tree in which the sap had run dry a generation before. As he stood there he heard a sound, and turned his face toward it, a sound that came from a mass of tumbled boulders, like the falling of a small rock upon a larger one. And as he looked there came from the darkness of the boulders a flash of fire and the explosion of a gun, and as Mukoki crumpled down in his tracks there followed a cry so terrible, so unhuman, so blood-curdling that, as he fell, an answering cry of horror burst from the lips of the old warrior. He lay like dead, though he was not touched. Instinct more than reason had impelled him to fall at the sound of the mysterious shot. Cautiously he wormed his rifle to his shoulder. But there came no movement from the rocks.

Then, from half-way down the mountain, there came again that terrible cry, and Mukoki knew that no animal in all these wilds could make it, but that it was human, and yet more savage than anything that had ever brought terror into his soul. Trembling, he crouched to the earth, a nameless fear chilling the blood in his veins. And the cry came again, and yet again, always farther and farther away, now at the foot of the mountain, now upon the plain, now floating away toward the chasm, echoing and reechoing between the mountain ridges, startling the creatures of the night into silence, and wresting deep sobbing breaths from out of Mukoki's soul. And the old warrior moved not a muscle until far away, miles and miles, it seemed, there died the last echo of it, and only the whispering winds rustled over the mountain top.

CHAPTER XI

THE CRY IN THE CHASM

If Mukoki had been a white man he would have analyzed in some way the meaning of those strange cries. But the wild and its savage things formed his world; and his world, until this night, had never known human or beast that could make the terrible sounds he had heard. So for an hour he crouched where he had fallen, still trembling with that nameless fear, and trying hard to form a solution of what had happened. Slowly he recovered himself. For many years he had mingled with white people at the Post and reason now battled with the superstitions of his race.

He had been fired at. He had heard the whistling song of the ball over his head, and had heard it strike the tree behind him. For a time those rocks toward which he stared like fascinated beast had concealed a man. But what kind of man! He remembered the ancient battle-cries of his tribe, and of the enemies of his tribe, but none was like the cries that had followed the shot. He heard them still; they rang in his ears, and sent shivering chills up his back. And the more he tried to reason the greater that nameless fear grew in him, until he slunk like an animal down the side of the mountain, through the dip, and out again upon the plain. And with that same nameless fear always close behind him, urging him on with its terrors, he sped back over the trail that he had followed that day, nor for an instant did he stop to rest until he came to the camp-fire of Rod and Wabigoon.

Usually an Indian hides his fears; he conceals them as a white man does his sins. But to-night Mukoki's experience had passed beyond the knowledge of his race, and he told of what had happened, trembling still, cringing when a great white rabbit darted close to the fire. Rod and Wabi listened to him in mute astonishment.

"Could it have been a Woonga?" asked Wabi.

"No Woonga," replied the old warrior quickly, shaking his head.
"Woonga no mak' noise lak that!"

He drew away from the fire, wrapped himself in a blanket, and crept into the shelter that Rod and Wabigoon had built. The two boys looked at each other in silence.

"Muky has certainly had some most extraordinary adventure," said Wabi at last. "I have never seen him like this before. It is easy to guess the meaning of the shot. Some of the Woongas may still be in the country, and one of them saw Mukoki, and fired at him. But the scream! What do you make of that?"

"Do you suppose," whispered Rod, speaking close to his companion's ear, "that Mukoki's imagination helped him out to-night?" He paused for a moment as he saw the look of disapproval in Wabigoon's eyes, and then went on. "I don't mean to hint that he stretched his story purposely. He was standing on the mountain top. Suddenly there came a flash of fire, the report of a rifle, and a bullet zipped close to his head. And at that same instant, or a moment later—well, you remember the scream of the lynx!"

"You believe that it might have been a lynx, startled by the shot, and sent screaming across the plain?"

"Yes."

"Impossible. At the sound of that shot a lynx would have remained as still as death!"

"Still there are always exceptions," persisted the white youth.

"Not in the case of lynx," declared Wabigoon. "No animal made those cries. Mukoki is as fearless as a lion. The cry of a lynx would have stirred his blood with pleasure instead of fear. Whatever the sounds were they turned Mukoki's blood into water. They made him a coward, and he ran, ran, mind you! until he got back to us! Is that like Mukoki? I tell you the cries—"

"What?"

"Were something very unusual," finished Wabigoon quietly, rising to his feet "Perhaps we will find out more to-morrow. As it is, I believe we had better stand guard in camp to-night. I will go to bed now and you can awaken me after a while."

Wabigoon's words and the strangeness of his manner put Rod ill at ease, despite his arguments of a few moments before, and no sooner did he find himself alone beside the fire than he began to be filled with an unpleasant premonition of lurking danger. For a time he sat very still, trying to peer into the shadows beyond the fire and listening to the sounds that came to him from out of the night. As he watched and listened his brain worked ceaselessly, conjuring picture after picture of what that danger might be, and at last he drew out of the firelight and concealed himself in the deep gloom of the bush. From here he could see the camp, and at the same time was safe from a possible rifle shot.

The night passed with tedious slowness, and he was glad when, a little after midnight, Wabi came out to relieve him. At dawn he was in turn awakened by the young Indian. Mukoki was already up and had prepared his pack. Apparently he had regained his old spirits, but both Rod and Wabigoon could see that behind them the fear of the preceding night still haunted him. That morning he did not set off ahead of the two boys with his pack but walked beside them, stopping to rest when they lowered their canoe, his eyes never ceasing their sharp scrutiny of the plain and distant ridges. Once when Mukoki mounted a big rock to look about him, Wabi whispered,

"I tell you it's strange, Rod—mighty strange!"

An hour later the old warrior halted and threw off his load. The three had approached within a quarter of a mile of the dip in the mountain.

"Leave canoe here," he said. "Go lak fox to old camp. Mebbe see!"

He took the lead now, followed closely by the boys. The safety of the old pathfinder's rifle was down, and following his example Rod and Wabigoon held their own guns in readiness for instant fire. As they neared the summit of the ridge on which Mukoki's life had been attempted the suspense of the two young hunters became almost painfully acute. Mukoki's actions not only astonished them, but set their blood tingling with his own strange fear. Many times had Wabigoon seen his faithful comrade in moments of deadly peril but never, even when the Woongas were close upon their trail, had he known him to take them as seriously as he did the ascent of this mountain. Every few steps Mukoki paused, listening and watchful. Not the smallest twig broke under his moccasined feet; the movement of the smallest bird, the trembling of a bush, the scurry of a rabbit halted him, rigid, his rifle half to shoulder. And Rod and Wabigoon soon become filled with this same panic-stricken fear. What terrible dread was it that filled Mukoki's soul? Had he seen something of which he had not told them? Did he think something which he had not revealed?

Foot by foot the three came to the top of the ridge. There Mukoki straightened himself, and stood erect. There were no signs of a living creature about them. Down in the dip nestled the little lake, gleaming in the midday sun. They could make out the debris of the burned cabin in which they had passed their hunting season, and close to this was the pack which Mukoki had dropped there the night before. No one had molested it. Wabi's face relaxed. Rod, breathing easier, laughed softly. What had there been to fear? He glanced questioningly at Mukoki.

"There rocks, there tree," said the old warrior, in answer to Rod's glance, "down there went scream!" He pointed far out across the plain.

Wabi had gone to the tree.

"See here, Rod!" he cried. "By George, this was a close shave!" He pointed to a tiny hole freshly made in the smooth white surface of the tree as the others came up. "There—stand there, Mukoki, back to the tree, as you said you were when the shot was fired. Great Caesar, that fellow had a dead line on your head—two inches high! No wonder it made you think the scream of a lynx was something else!"

"No lynx," said Mukoki, his face darkening.

"Shame on you, Muky!" laughed Wabigoon. "Don't get angry. I won't say it again if it makes you mad."

Rod had drawn his hunting-knife and was prodding the point of it in the bullet hole.

"I can feel the ball," he said. "It's not in more than an inch."

"That's curious," exclaimed Wabigoon, coming close beside him. "It ought to be half-way through the tree at least! Eh, Muky? I don't believe it would have hurt—"

He stopped. Rod had turned with a sudden excited cry. He held out his knife, tip upward, and pointed to it with the index finger of his free hand. Wabi's eyes fell on the tip of the blade. Mukoki stared. For a full half minute the three stood in speechless amazement. Clinging to the knife tip was a tiny fleck of yellow, gleaming lustrously in the sun as Rod slowly turned the handle of his weapon.

"Another—gold—bullet!"

The words fell from Wabi's lips very slowly, and so low that they were scarce above a whisper. Mukoki seemed to have ceased breathing. Rod's eyes met the old warrior's.

"What does it mean?"

Wabi had pulled his knife and was digging into the tree. A few deep cuts and the golden bullet lay exposed to view.

"What does it mean?" repeated the white youth.

Again he addressed his question to Mukoki.

"Man who shoot bear—heem no dead," replied the old pathfinder. "Same gun, same gold, same—"

"Same what?"

A strange gleam came for an instant into Mukoki's eyes, and without finishing he turned and pointed across the narrow plain that lay between them and the mysterious chasm which they were to follow in their search for treasure.

"Cry went there!" he said shortly.

"To the chasm!" said Wabi.

"To the chasm!" repeated Rod.

Impelled by the same thought the three adventurers went toward the rocks from which the shot had been fired. Surely they would discover some sign there, or lower down upon the plain, where the melting snows had softened the earth. Mukoki led in the search, and foot by foot they examined the spot where the mysterious marksman must have stood when he sent his golden bullet so close to the Indian's head.

But not a trace of his presence had he left behind. Working abreast, the three began the descent of the ridge. Hardly had they covered a third of the distance to the plain when Wabi, who was trailing between Rod and the old Indian, called out that he had made a discovery. Mukoki had already reached him when Rod came up, and the two were gazing silently at something fluttering from a bush.

"Lynx hair!" cried Rod. "A lynx has been this way!" He could not entirely conceal the triumph in his voice. He had been right in his conjecture of the night before, the cry that had frightened Mukoki had been made by a lynx!

"Yes, a lynx has been this way, a lynx four feet high," said Wabigoon quietly, and the touch of raillery in his voice assured Rod that he had still other lessons to learn in the life of this big wilderness. "Lynx don't grow that big, Rod!"

"Then it's—" Rod feared to go on.

"Lynx fur. That's just what it is. Whoever fired at Mukoki last night was dressed in skins! Now, can you tell us what that means?"

Without waiting for an answer Wabigoon resumed his search. But the mountain side gave no further evidence. Not a footprint was found upon the plain. If the mysterious person who had fired the golden bullet had leaped from the mountain top into space he could have left no fewer traces behind him. At the end of an hour Rod and his companions returned to the canoe, carried their loads to the pack in the dip, and prepared dinner. Their suspense and fear, and specially Mukoki's dread, were in a large measure gone. But at the same time they were more hopelessly mystified than ever. That there was danger ahead of them, that the menace of golden bullets was actual and thrilling, all three were well agreed, but the sunlight of day and a little sound reasoning had dispelled their half superstitious terrors of the previous night and they began to face the new situation with their former confidence.

"We can't let this delay us," said Wabi, as they ate their dinner. "By night we ought to be in our old camp at the head of the chasm, where we held the Woongas at bay last winter. The sooner we get out of the way of these golden bullets the better it will be for us!"

Mukoki shrugged his shoulders.

"Gold bullet follow, I guess so," he grunted, "Cry went there—to chasm!"

"I don't believe this fellow, whoever he is, will hang to our trail," continued Wabi, giving Rod a suggestive look. A few moments later he found an opportunity to whisper, "We've got to get that cry out of Muky's head, Rod, or we'll never find our gold!"

When Mukoki had gone to arrange his pack the young Indian spoke earnestly to his companion.

"Muky isn't afraid of bullets, either gold or lead; he isn't afraid of any danger on earth. But that cry haunts him. He is trying not to let us know, yet it haunts him just the same. Do you know what he is thinking? No? Well, I do! He is superstitious, like the rest of his race, and the two gold bullets, the terrible cries, and the fact that we found no tracks upon the plain are all carrying him toward one conclusion, that the strange thing that fired at him is—"

Wabigoon paused and wiped his face, and it was easy for Rod to see that he was suppressing some unusual excitement.

"What does he think it is?"

"I'm not sure, not quite sure, yet," went on the Indian youth. "But listen! It is a legend in Mukoki's tribe, and always has been, that once in every so many generations they are visited by a terrible warrior sent by the Great Spirit who takes sacrifice of them, a sacrifice of human life, because of a great wrong that was once done by their people. And this warrior, though invisible, has a voice that makes the mountains quake and the rivers stand still with fear, and in his great bow he shoots shafts that are made of gold! Do you understand? Last night I heard Mukoki talking about it in his sleep. Either we must hear this cry, and find out more about it, or hurry to a place where it won't be heard again. Golden bullets and cries and Mukoki's superstitions are going to be worse than Woongas if we don't watch out!"

"But the whole thing is as plain as day!" declared Rod in astonishment. "A man shot at the bear, and the same man shot at Mukoki, and he fired gold each time. Surely—"

"It's not the man part of it," interrupted the other. "It's the cry.
There, Mukoki has his pack ready. Let's start for the chasm at once!"

This time the boys had a heavier burden than usual, for in the canoe they placed one of the two loads carried by Mukoki, and consequently their progress toward the chasm was much slower than that across the plain. It was late in the afternoon when they reached the break that led into the chasm, and as they cautiously made the descent now Rod thought of the thrilling pursuit of the Woonga horde, and how a few weeks before they had discovered this break just in time for Wabi and him to save their lives, and that of the wounded Mukoki. It was with a feeling almost of awe that the three adventurers penetrated deeper and deeper into the silent gloom of this mystery-filled gulch between the mountains, and when they reached the bottom they set their loads down without speaking, their eyes roving over the black walls of rock, their hearts throbbing a little faster with excitement.

For here, at this break in the mountain, began the romantic trail drawn by men long dead, the trail that led to a treasure of gold.

As the three sat in silence, the gloom in the chasm thickened. The sun had passed beyond the southwestern forests, and through the narrow rift between the mountain walls there fell but the ebbing light of day, dissolving itself into the shadows of dusk as it struggled weakly in the cavernous depths. For a few minutes this swift fading of day into night gripped the adventurers in its spell. What did the lonely solitudes of that chasm hold for them? Where would they lead them? To Rod's mind there came a picture of the silver fox and a thought of his dream, when for a few miles he had explored the mysteries of this strange, sunless world shut in by rock walls. Again he saw the dancing skeletons, heard the rattle of their bones, and watched the wonderful dream-battle that had led him to the birch-bark map. Wabigoon, his eyes gleaming in the gathering darkness, thought of their flight from the outlaw savages, and Mukoki—

The white youth had turned a little to look at the old warrior. Mukoki sat as rigid as a pillar of stone an arm's reach from him. Head erect, arms tense, his eyes gleaming strangely, he stared straight out into the gloom between the chasm walls. Rod shivered. He knew, knew without questioning, that Mukoki was thinking of the cry!

And at that instant there floated up from the black chaos ahead a sound, a sound low and weird, like the moaning of a winter's wind through the pine tops, swelling, advancing, until it ended in a shriek—a shriek that echoed and reëchoed between the chasm walls, dying away in a wail that froze the blood of the three who sat and listened!

CHAPTER XII

WABI MAKES A STRANGE DISCOVERY

Mukoki broke the silence which followed the terrible cry. With a choking sound, as if some unseen hand were clutching at his throat, he slipped from the rock upon which he was sitting and crouched behind it, his rifle gleaming faintly as he leveled it down the chasm. There came the warning click of Wabigoon's gun, and the young Indian hunched himself forward until he was no more than an indistinct shadow in the fast-deepening gloom of night. Only Rod still sat erect. For a moment his heart seemed to stand still. Then something leaped into his brain and spread like fire through his veins, calling him to his feet, trembling with the knowledge of what that cry had told him! It was not a lesson from the wilderness that Roderick Drew was learning now. As fast as the mind could travel he had gone far back into the strife and misery and madness of civilization, and there he found the language of that fearful cry floating up the chasm. He had heard it once, twice—yes, again and again, and the memory of it had burned deep down into his soul. He turned to his companions, trying to speak, but the horror that had first filled Mukoki now fastened itself on him, and his tongue was lifeless.

"A madman!"

Wabi's fingers dug into his arm like the claws of a bear.

"A what!"

"A madman!" repeated Rod, trying to speak more calmly. "The man who shot the bear and fired at Mukoki and who uses gold bullets in his gun is mad—raving mad! I have heard those screams before—in the Eloise insane asylum, near Detroit. He's—"

The words were frozen on his lips. Again the cry echoed up the chasm. It was nearer this time, and with a sobbing, terrified sound, something that Wabi had never heard fall from Mukoki's lips before, the old warrior clung to Roderick's arm. Darkness hid the terror in his face, but the white boy could feel it in the grip of his hands.

"Mad, raving mad!" he cried. Suddenly he gripped Mukoki fiercely by the shoulders, and as Wabigoon crouched forward, ready to fire at the first movement in the gloom, he thrust the butt of his rifle in his back. "Don't shoot!" he commanded. "Mukoki, don't be a fool! That's a man back there, a man who has suffered and starved, starved, mind you!—until he's mad, stark mad! It would be worse than murder to kill him!"

He stopped, and Mukoki drew back a step, breathing deeply.

"Heem—starve—no eat—gone bad dog?" he questioned softly. In an instant Wabi was at his side.

"That's it, Muky—he's gone bad dog, just like that husky of ours who went bad because he swallowed a fish bone. White men sometimes go bad dog when they are thirsty and starving!"

"Our Great Spirit tells us that we must never harm them," added Rod. "We put them in big houses, larger than all of the houses at the Post together, and feed them and clothe them and care for them all their lives. Are you afraid of a bad dog, Muky, or of a man who has gone bad dog?"

"Bad dog bite deep—mebby so we kill heem!"

"But we don't kill them until we have to," persisted the quick-witted Wabigoon, who saw the way in which Rod's efforts were being directed. "Didn't we save our husky by taking the fish bone out of his throat? We must save this bad dog, because he is a white man, like Rod. He thinks all men are his enemies, just as a bad dog thinks all other dogs are his enemies. So we must be careful and not give him a chance to shoot us but we mustn't harm him!"

"It will be best if we don't let him know we are in the chasm," said Rod, still speaking for Mukoki's benefit. "He's probably going out on the plain, and must climb up this break in, the mountain. Let's move our stuff a little out of his path."

As the two boys went to the canoe their hands touched. Wabi was startled by the coldness of his friend's fingers.

"We've fixed Mukoki," he whispered. "He won't shoot. But—"

"We may have to," replied Rod. "That will be up to you and me, Wabi. We must use judgment, and unless it's a case of life or death—"

"Ugh!" shuddered the young Indian.

"If he doesn't discover our presence to-night we will get out of his way to-morrow," continued Rod. "No fire—no talking. We must be as still as death!"

For some time after their outfit was concealed among the rocks Wabigoon sat with his mouth close to the old pathfinder's ear. Then he returned to Rod.

"Muky understands. He has never seen or heard of a madman, and it is hard for him to comprehend. But he knows—now, and understands what he must do."

"Sh-h-h-h-h!"

"What is it?"

"I thought I heard a sound!" breathed Rod. "Did you hear it?"

"No."

The two listened. There was an awesome silence in the chasm now, broken only by the distant murmur of running water, a strange, chilling stillness in which the young hunters could hear the excited beating of their own hearts. To Roderick the minutes passed like so many hours. His ears were keyed to the highest tension of expectancy, his eyes stared into the gloom beyond them until they ached with his efforts to see. At every instant he expected to hear again that terrible scream, this time very near, and he prepared himself to meet it. But the seconds passed, and then the minutes, and still there came no quick running of mad footsteps, no repetition of the cry. Had the madman turned the other way? Was he plunging deeper into the blackness of this mysterious world of his between the mountains?

"I guess I was mistaken," he whispered softly to Wabigoon. "Shall we get out our blankets?"

"We might as well make ourselves comfortable," replied the young Indian. "You sit here, and listen while I undo the pack."

He went noiselessly to Mukoki, who was leaning against the pack, and Rod could hear them fumbling at the straps on the bundle. After a little Wabi returned and the two boys spread out their blankets beside the rock upon which they had been sitting. But there was no thought of sleep in the mind of either, though both were dead tired from their long day's work. They sat closer together, shoulder touching shoulder, and unknown to his companion Roderick drew his revolver, cocked it silently and placed it where he could feel the cold touch of its steel between his fingers. He knew that he was the only one of the three who fully realized the horror of their situation.

Mukoki's mind, simple in its reasoning of things that did not belong to the wilderness, had accepted the assurances and explanations of Rod and Wabigoon. Wabi, half-bred in the wild, felt alarm only in the sense of physical peril. It was different with the white youth. What is there in civilization that sends the chill of terror to one's heart more quickly than the presence of a human being who has gone mad? And this madman was at large! At that very instant he might be listening to their breathing and their whispered words half a dozen feet away; any moment might see the blackness take form and the terrible thing hurl itself at their throats. Rod, unlike Wabigoon, knew that the powers of this strange creature of the chasm were greater than their own, that it could travel with the swiftness and silence of an animal through the darkness, that perhaps it could smell them and feel their presence as it passed on its way to the plain. He was anxious now to hear the cry again. What was the meaning of this silence? Was the madman already conscious of their presence? Was he creeping upon them at that moment, as still as the black shadows that shut in their vision? His mind was working in such vivid imaginings that he was startled when Wabi prodded him gently in the side.

"Look over there—across the chasm," he whispered. "See that glow on the mountain wall?"

"The moon!" replied Rod.

"Yes. I've been watching it, and it's creeping down and down. The moon is going to swing across this break in the mountains. In fifteen minutes we shall be able to see."

"It won't swing across so much as it will come up in line with us," replied Rod. "Watch how that light is lengthening! We shall be able to see for several hours."

He started to rise to his feet but fell back with an astonished cry. For a third time there came the mad hunter's scream, this time far above and beyond them, floating down from the distance of the moon-lit plain!

"He passed us!" exclaimed Wabi. "He passed us—and we didn't hear him!" He leaped to his feet and his voice rose excitedly until it rang in a hundred echoes between the chasm walls. "He passed us, and we didn't hear him!"

Mukoki's voice came strangely from out of the gloom.

"No man do that! No man—no man—"

"Hush!" commanded Rod. "Now is our time, boys! Quick, get everything to the creek. He's half a mile out on the plain and we can get away before he comes back. I'd rather risk a few rocks than another one of his golden bullets!"

"So had I!" cried Wabi.

As if their lives depended on their exertions the three set to work. Mukoki staggered ahead over the rocks with his burden while the boys followed with the light canoe and the remaining pack. Their previous experiences in the chasm had taught them where to approach the stream, and ten minutes later they were at its side. Without a moment's hesitation Mukoki dropped his pack and plunged in. The edge of the moon was just appearing over the southern mountain wall and by its light Rod and Wabigoon could see that the water of the creek was rushing with great swiftness as high as the old warrior's knees.

"No ver' deep," said the Indian. "Rocks—"

"I followed this creek for half a dozen miles and its bottom is as smooth as a floor!" interrupted Rod. "There's no danger of rocks for that distance!"

He made no effort now to suppress the pleasure which he felt at the escape from their unpleasant situation. Mukoki steadied the canoe as it was placed in the water, and was the last to climb into it, taking his usual position in the stern where he could use to best advantage the powerful sweeps of his paddle. In an instant the swift current of the little stream caught the birch bark and carried it along with remarkable speed. After several futile strokes of his paddle Wabi settled back upon his heels.

"It's all up to you, Muky," he called softly. "I can't do a thing from the bow. The current is too swift. All you can do is to keep her nose straight."

The light of the moon was now filling the chasm and the adventurers could see distinctly for a hundred yards or more ahead of them. Each minute seemed to add to the swiftness and size of the stream, and by the use of his paddle Wabi found that it was constantly deepening, until he could no longer touch bottom. Rod's eyes were ceaselessly on the alert for familiar signs along the shore. He was sure that he knew when they passed the spot where he killed the silver fox, and he called Wabi's attention to it. Then the rocks sped past with increasing swiftness, and as the moon rose higher the three could see where the overflowing torrent sent out little streams that twisted and dashed themselves into leaping foam in the wildness of the chasm beyond the main channel. These increased in number and size as the journey continued, until Mukoki began to feel the influence of their currents and called on Wabi and Rod for assistance. Suddenly Rod gave a muffled shout as they shot past a mass of huge boulders on their right.

"That's where I camped the night I dreamed of the skeletons!" he cried. "I don't know what the stream is like from here on. Be careful!"

Wabi gave a terrific lunge with his paddle and the cone of a black rock hissed past half a canoe length away.

"It's as black as a dungeon ahead, and I can hear rocks!" he shouted.
"Bring her in if you can, Muky, bring her in!"

There came the sudden sharp crack of snapping wood and a low exclamation of alarm fell from Mukoki. His paddle had broken at the shaft. In a flash Rod realized what had happened and passed back his own, but that moment's loss of time proved almost fatal. Freed of its guiding hand the birch bark swung broadside to the current, and at the same time Wabi's voice rose in a shrill cry of warning.

"It's not rocks, it's a whirlpool!" he yelled. "The other shore, swing her out, swing her out!"

He dug his own paddle deep down into the racing current and from behind Mukoki exerted his most powerful efforts, but it was too late! A hundred feet ahead the stream tore between two huge rocks as big as houses, and just beyond these Rod caught a glimpse of frothing water churning itself milk-white in the moonlight. But it was only a glimpse. With a velocity that was startling the canoe shot between the rocks, and as a choking sea of spray leaped into their faces Wabigoon's voice came back again in a loud command for the others to hang to the gunwales of their frail craft. For an instant, in which his thoughts seemed to have left him, a roaring din filled Rod's ears; a white, churning mist hid everything but his own arms and clutching hands, and then the birch bark darted with the sudden impetus of a freshly-shot arrow around the jagged edge of the boulder—and he could see again.

Here was the whirlpool! More than once Wabi had told him of these treacherous traps, made by the mountain streams, and of the almost certain death that awaited the unlucky canoe man drawn into their smothering embrace. There was no angry raging of the flood here; at first it seemed to Rod that they were floating almost without motion upon a black, lazy sea that made neither sound nor riffle. Scarce half a dozen canoe lengths away he saw the white center of the maelstrom, and there came to his ears above the dash of the stream between the two great rocks a faint hissing sound that curdled the blood in his veins, the hissing of the treacherous undertow that would soon drag them to their death! In the passing of a thought there flashed into the white youth's mind a story that Mukoki had told him of an Indian who had been lost in one of these whirlpools of the spring floods, and whose body had been tossed and pitched about in its center for more than a week. For the first time the power of speech came to him.

"Shall we jump?" he shouted.

"Hang to the canoe."

Wabi fairly shrieked the words, and yet as he spoke he drew himself half erect, as if about to leap into the flood. The momentum gathered in its swift rush between the rocks had carried their frail craft almost to the outer edge of the deadly trap, and as this momentum ceased and the canoe yielded to the sucking forces of the maelstrom the young Indian shrieked out his warning again.

"Hang to the canoe!"

The words were scarcely out of his mouth when he stood erect and launched himself like an animal into the black depths toward shore. With a terrified cry Rod rose to his knees. In another instant he would have plunged recklessly after Wabi, but Mukoki's voice sounding behind him, snarling in its fierceness, stopped him.

"Hang to canoe!"

There came a jerk. The bow of the canoe swung inward and the stern whirled so quickly that Rod, half kneeling, nearly lost his balance. In that instant he turned his face and saw the old warrior standing, as Wabigoon had done before him, and as Mukoki leaped there came for a third time that warning cry:

"Hang to canoe!"

And Rod hung. He knew that for some reason those commands were meant for him, and him alone; he knew that the desperate plunges of his comrades were not inspired by cowardice or fear, but not until the birch bark ground upon the shore and he tumbled out in safety did he fully comprehend what had happened. Holding the rope with which they tied their canoe, Wabigoon had taken a desperate chance. His quick mind had leaped like a flash of powder to their last hope, and at the crucial moment, just as the momentum of the birch bark gave way to the whirling forces of the pool, he had jumped a good seven feet toward shore, and had found bottom! Another twelve inches of water under him and all would have been lost.

Wabigoon stood panting and dripping wet, and in the moonlight his face was as white as the tub-like spot of foam out in the center of the maelstrom.

"That's what you call going to kingdomcome and getting out again!" he gasped. "Muky, that was the closest shave we've ever had! It has your avalanche beaten to a frazzle!"

Mukoki was dragging the canoe upon the pebbly shore, and still overcome by the suddenness of all that had happened Rod went to his assistance.

The adventurers now discovered themselves in a most interesting situation. The night had indeed been one of curious and thrilling happenings for them, and here was a pretty climax to it all! They had escaped the mad hunter by running into the almost fatal grip of the whirlpool, and now they had escaped the perils of that seething death-trap by plunging into a tiny rock-bound prison which seemed destined to hold them for all time, or at least until the floods of spring subsided. Straight above them, and shutting them in entirely, rose precipitous rock walls. On the only open side was the deadly maelstrom.

Even Mukoki as he glanced about him was struck by the humor of their situation, and chuckled softly.

Wabi stood with his hands deep in his soaked pockets, facing the moonlit walls. Then he turned to Rod, and grinned; then he faced the whirlpool, and after that his eyes swept the space of sky above them. The situation was funny, at first; but when he looked at the white youth again the smile had died out of his face.

"Wouldn't that madman have fun if he found us now!" he whispered.

Mukoki was traveling slowly around the rock walls. The space in which they were confined was not more than fifty feet in diameter, and there was not even a crack by means of which a squirrel might have found exit. The prison was perfect. The old pathfinder came back and sat down with a grunt.

"We might as well have supper and a good sleep," suggested Rod, who was hungry. "Surely we need fear no attack from beast or man to-night!"

At least there was this consolation, and the gold hunters ate a hearty meal of cold bear meat and prepared for slumber. The night was unusually warm, and both Mukoki and Wabigoon hung out their wet clothes to dry while they slept in their blankets. Rod did not open his eyes again until Wabi awakened him in the morning. Both Indians were dressed and it was evident that they had been up for some time. When Rod went to the water to wash himself he was surprised to find all of their supplies repacked in the canoe, as though their journey was about to be resumed immediately after breakfast, and when he returned to where Mukoki and Wabigoon had placed their food on a flat stone in the center of what he had regarded as their prison, he observed that both of his companions were in an unusually cheerful frame of mind.

"Looks as though you expected to get out of here pretty soon," he said, nodding toward the canoe.

"So we do!" responded Wabi. "We're going to take a swim through the whirlpool!"

He laughed at the incredulity in Rod's face.

"That is, we're going to navigate along the edge of it," he amended. "Muky and I have tied together every bit of rope and strap in our outfit, even to our gun-slings, and we've got a piece about eighty feet long. We'll show you how to use it after breakfast."

It took but a few minutes to dispose of the rather unappetizing repast of cold bear meat, biscuits and water. Wabi then led the way to the extreme edge of the great rock which formed the eastern wall of their prison, waded in the water to his knees, and directed Rod's gaze to a point of land jutting out into the stream about sixty feet beyond the rock.

"If we can reach that," explained Wabi, "we can portage around the rest of the whirlpool to the main channel. The water is very deep along the edge of this rock, but the undertow doesn't seem to have any great force. I believe that we can make it. The experiment won't be a dangerous one at any rate."

The canoe was now dragged to the edge of the rock and launched, Mukoki taking his place in the stern while Wabigoon placed Rod a little ahead of the midship rib.

"You must paddle on your left side, every minute and as fast as you can," advised the young Indian. "I am to remain behind, holding one end of this rope, so that if you are drawn toward the maelstrom I can pull you back. Understand?"

"Yes—but you. How—"

"Oh, I'll swim!" said Wabi in rank bravado. "I don't mind a little whirlpool like that at all!"

Mukoki chuckled in high humor, and Roderick asked no more questions, but at Wabi's command dug in his paddle and kept at it until the birch bark safely made the point of land beyond the rock. When he looked back Wabi had tied the rope around his body and was already waist deep in the water. At a signal from Mukoki the young Indian plunged fearlessly into the edge of the whirlpool and like a great floundering fish he was quickly pulled across to safety. Most of his clothes had been brought over in the canoe, and after Wabigoon had exchanged his wet garments for these the adventurers were ready to continue their journey down the chasm. A short portage brought them to the main channel of the stream, where they once more launched their birch bark.

"If the whole trip is as exciting as this we'll never reach our gold," said Wabi, as they slipped out into the swift current. "A madman, a whirlpool and a prison, all in one night, is almost more than we can stand."

"There's a good deal of truth in the old saying that it never rains but it pours," replied Rod. "Maybe we'll have smooth sailing from now on."

"Mebby!" grunted the old pathfinder from behind.

Rod's optimism was vindicated for that day, at least. Until noon the canoe sped swiftly down the chasm without mishap. The stream, to which each mile added its contribution of flood water from the mountain tops, increased constantly in width and depth, but only now and then was there a rock to threaten their progress, and no driftwood at all. When the gold seekers landed for dinner they were confident of two things: that they had passed far beyond the mad hunter's reach, and were very near to the first waterfall. Memory of the thrilling experiences through which they had so recently run the gauntlet was replaced by the most exciting anticipation of the sound and sight of that first waterfall, which was so vitally associated with their search for the lost treasure. This time a hearty dinner was cooked, and it took more than an hour to prepare and eat it.

When the journey was resumed Mukoki placed himself in the bow, his sharp eyes scanning the rocks and mountain walls ahead of him. Two hours after the start he gave an exultant exclamation, and raised a warning hand above his head. The three listened. Faintly above the rush of the swift current there came to their ears the distant rumble of falling water!

Forgetful now of the madman back in the chasm, oblivious of everything but the fact that they had at last reached the first of the three falls which were to lead them to the gold, Wabi gave a whoop that echoed and reëchoed between the mountain walls, and Rod joined him with all the power of his lungs. Mukoki grinned, chuckled in his curious way, and a few moments later signaled Wabi to guide the canoe ashore.

"We portage here," he explained. "Current swift there—mebby go over fall!"

A short carry of two or three hundred yards brought them to the cataract. It was, as Mukoki had said after his long trip of exploration a few months before, a very small fall, not more than a dozen feet in height. But over it there was now rushing a thundering deluge of water. An easy trail led to the stream below it, and no time was lost in getting under way again.

Although they had traveled fully forty miles since morning, the day had been an easy and most interesting one for the three adventurers. On the swift current of the chasm stream they had worked but little, and the ceaseless change of scenery in this wonderful break between the mountain ridges held an ever-increasing fascination for them. Late in the afternoon, the course changed from its northeasterly direction to due north, and at this point there was an ideal spot for camping. Over an extent of an acre or more there was a sweeping hollow of fine white sand, with great quantities of dry wood cluttering the edge of the depression.

"That's a curious spot!" said Wabi as they drew up their canoe. "Looks like—"

"A lake," grunted Mukoki. "Long time ago—a lake."

"The curve of the stream right here has swept up so much sand that the water can't get into it," added Rod, looking the place over.

Wabi had gone a few paces back. Suddenly he stopped, and with a half shout he gesticulated excitedly to his companions. Something in his manner took Rod and Mukoki to him on the run.

When they came up the Indian youth stood mutely pointing at something in the sand.

Clearly imprinted in that sand was the shape of a human foot, a foot that had worn neither boot nor moccasin when it left its trail in the lake bed, but which was as naked as the quivering hand which Wabigoon now held toward it!

And from that single footprint the eyes of the astonished adventurers traveled quickly to a hundred others, until it seemed to them that a dozen naked savages must have been dancing in these sands only a few hours before.

And Rod, glancing toward the driftwood, saw something else,—something toward which he pointed, speechless, white with that same strange excitement that had taken possession of Wabigoon!

CHAPTER XIII

THE THIRD WATERFALL

The others followed Rod's arm. Behind him he heard the gentle click of Wabigoon's revolver and the sharp, vicious snap of the safety on Mukoki's rifle.

From beyond the driftwood there was rising a thin spiral of smoke!

"Whoever they are, they have certainly seen or heard us!" said Wabi, after they had stood in silence for a full minute.

"Unless they are gone from camp," replied Rod in a whisper.

"Keep eyes open!" warned Mukoki as they advanced cautiously in the direction of the smoke. "No can tell what, I guess so!"

He was first to mount the driftwood, and then he gave vent to a huge grunt. The smoke was rising from beside a charred log which was heaped half-way up its side with ashes and earth. In a flash the meaning of the ash and dirt dawned on Rod and his companions. The fire was banked. Those who had built it were gone, but they expected to return. The naked footprints were thick about the camp-fire, and close to one end of the charred log were scattered a number of bones. One after another Mukoki picked up several of these and closely examined them. While Rod and Wabigoon were still gazing about them in blank astonishment, half expecting attack from a savage horde at any moment, the old warrior had already reached a conclusion, and calling to his companions he brought their attention to the tracks in the sand.

"Same feet!" he exclaimed. "One man mak' all track!"

"Impossible!" cried Wabi. "There are—thousands of them!"

Mukoki grunted and fell upon his knees.

"Heem big toe—right foot—broke sometime. Same in all track. See?"

Disgusted at his own lack of observation, Wabigoon saw at once that the old pathfinder was right. The joint of the big toe on the right foot was twisted fully half an inch outward, a deformity that left a peculiar impression in the sand, and every other track bore this telltale mark. No sooner were the two boys convinced of the correctness of Mukoki's assertion than another and still more startling surprise was sprung on them. Holding out his handful of bones, Mukoki said:

"Meat no cook—eat raw!"

"Great Scott!" gasped Rod.

Wabi's eyes flashed with a new understanding, and as he gazed into Rod's astonished face the latter, too, began to comprehend the significance of it all.

"It must have been the madman!"

"Yes."

"And he was here yesterday!"

"Probably the day before," said Wabi. The young Indian turned suddenly to Mukoki. "What did he want of the fire if he didn't cook meat?" he asked.

Mukoki shrugged his shoulders but did not answer.

"Well, it wasn't cooked, anyway," declared Wabi, again examining the bones. "Here are chunks of raw flesh clinging to the bones. Perhaps he just singed the outside of his meat."

The old Indian nodded at this suggestion and turned to investigate the fire. On the end of the log were two stones, one flat and the other round and smooth, and after a moment's inspection of these he dropped an exclamation which was unusual for him, and which he used only in those rare intervals when all other language seemed to fail him.

"Bad dog man—mak' bullet—here!" he called, holding out the stones. "See—gold—gold!"

The boys hurried to his side.

"See—gold!" he repeated excitedly.

In the center of the flat stone there was a gleaming yellow film. A single glance told the story. With the round stone for a hammer the mad hunter had pounded his golden bullets into shape upon the flat stone! There was no longer a doubt in their minds; they were in the madman's camp. That morning they had left this strange creature of the wilderness fifty miles away. But how far away was he now? The fire slumbering under its covering of ash and earth proved that he meant to return—and soon. Would he travel by night as well as by day? Was it possible that he was already close behind them?

"He travels with the swiftness of an animal," said Wabi, speaking in a low voice to Rod. "Perhaps he will return to-night!"

Mukoki overheard him and shook his head.

"Mak' heem through chasm in two day on snow-shoe," he declared, referring to his trip of exploration to the first waterfall over the snows of the previous winter. "No mak' in t'ree day over rock!"

"If Mukoki is satisfied, I am," said Rod. "We can pull up behind the driftwood on the farther edge of the lake bed."

Wabi made no objection, and the camp site was chosen. Strangely enough, with the discovery of the footprints, the fire, the picked bones and the stones with which the mad hunter had manufactured his golden bullets, Mukoki seemed to have lost all fear of the wild creature of the chasm. He was confident now that he had only a man to deal with, a man who had gone "bad dog," and his curiosity overcame his alarm. His assurance served to dispel the apprehension of his companions, and sleep came early to the tired adventurers. Nor did anything occur during the night to awaken them.

Soon after dawn the trip down the chasm stream was resumed. With the abrupt turning of the channel to the north, however, there was an almost immediate change in the topography of the country. Within an hour the precipitous walls of the mountains gave place to verdure-covered slopes, and now and then the gold seekers found themselves between plains that swept back for a mile or more on either side. Frequent signs of game were observed along the shores of the river and several times during the morning moose and caribou were seen in the distance. A few months before, when they had invaded the wilderness to hunt and trap, this country would have aroused the wildest enthusiasm among Rod and his friends, but now they gave but little thought to their rifles. That morning they had set out with the intention of reaching the second waterfall before dusk, and it was with disappointment rather than gladness that they saw the swift current of the chasm torrent change into the slower, steadier sweep of a stream that had now widened into a fair-sized river. According to the map the second fall was about fifty-five miles from the mad hunter's camp. Darkness found them still fifteen miles from where it should be.

Excitement kept Rod awake most of that night. Try as he would, he could not keep visions of the lost treasure out of his mind. The next day they would be far on their way to the third and last waterfall. And then—the gold! That they might not find it, that the passing of half a century or more might have obliterated all traces left by its ancient discoverers, never for a moment disturbed his belief.

He was the first awake the following morning, the first to take his place in the canoe. Every minute now his ears were keenly attuned for that distant sound of falling water. But hours passed without a sign of it. Noon came. They had traveled six hours and had covered twenty-five miles instead of fifteen! Where was the waterfall?

There was a little more of anxiety in Wabigoon's eyes when they resumed their journey after dinner. Again and again Rod looked at his map, figuring out the distances as drawn by John Ball, the murdered Englishman. Surely the second waterfall could not be far away now! And still hour after hour passed, and mile after mile slipped behind them, until the three knew that they had gone fully thirty miles beyond where the cataract should have been, if the map was right. Twilight was falling when they stopped for supper. For the last hour Mukoki had spoken no word. A feeling of gloom was on them all; without questioning, each knew what the fears of the others were.

Was it possible that, after all, they had not solved the secret of the mysterious map?

The more Rod thought of it the more his fears possessed him. The two men who fought and died in the old cabin were on their way to civilization. They were taking gold with them, gold which they meant to exchange for supplies. Would they, at the same time, dare to have in their possession a map so closely defining their trail as the rude sketch on the bit of birch bark? Was there not some strange key, known only to themselves, necessary to the understanding of that sketch?

Mukoki had taken his rifle and disappeared in the plain along the river, and for a long time after they had eaten their bear steak and drank their hot coffee Rod and Wabigoon sat talking in the glow of the camp-fire. The old warrior had been gone for about an hour when suddenly there came the report of a gun from far down the stream, which was quickly followed by two others—three in rapid succession. After an interval of a few seconds there sounded two other shots.

"The signal!" cried Rod. "Mukoki wants us!"

Wabigoon sprang to his feet and emptied the five shots of his magazine into the air.

"Listen!"

Hardly had the echoes died away when there came again the reports of Mukoki's rifle.

Without another word the two boys hurried to the canoe, which had not been unloaded.

"He's a couple of miles down-stream," said Wabi, as they shoved off. "I wonder what's the matter?"

"I can make a pretty good guess," replied Rod, his voice trembling with a new excitement. "He has found the second waterfall!"

The thought gave fresh strength to their aching arms and the canoe sped swiftly down the stream. Fifteen minutes later another shot signaled to them, this time not more than a quarter of a mile away, and Wabi responded to it with a loud shout. Mukoki's voice floated back in an answering halloo, but before the young hunters came within sight of their comrade another sound reached their ears,—the muffled roar of a cataract! Again and again the boys sent their shouts of joy echoing through the night, and above the tumult of their own voices they heard the old warrior calling on them to put into shore. Mukoki was waiting for them when they landed.

"This is big un!" he greeted. "Mak' much noise, much swift water!"

"Hurrah!" yelled Rod for the twentieth time, jumping up and down in his excitement.

"Hurrah!" cried Wabi.

And Mukoki chuckled, and grinned, and rubbed his leathery hands together in high glee.

At last, when they had somewhat cooled down, Wabi said:

"That John Ball was a pretty poor fellow at a guess, eh? What do you say, Rod?"

"Or else pretty clever," added Rod. "By George, I wonder if he had a reason for making his scale fifty miles or so out of the way?"

Wabi looked at him, only partly understanding.

"What do you mean?"

"I mean that our third waterfall is more than likely to be mighty close to this one! And if it is—well, John Ball had a reason, and a good one! If we strike the last fall to-morrow it will be pretty good proof that he drew the map in a way intended to puzzle somebody,—perhaps his two partners, who were just about to start for civilization."

"Muky, how far have we come?" asked Wabigoon.

"T'ree time first fall," replied the old Indian quickly.

"A hundred and fifty miles—in three days and one night. I don't believe that is far out of the way. Then, according to the map, we should still be a hundred miles from the third fall."

"And we're not more than twenty-five!" declared Rod confidently. "Let's build a fire and go to bed. We'll have enough to do to-morrow—hunting gold!" The fourth day's journey was begun before it was yet light. Breakfast was eaten in the glow of the camp-fire, and by the time dawn broke the adventurers were already an hour upon their way. Nothing but confidence now, animated them. The mad hunter and his golden bullets were entirely forgotten in these last hours of their exciting quest. Once, far back, Rod had thought with chilling dread that this might be the madman's trail, that his golden bullets might come from the treasure they were seeking. But he gave no thought to this possibility now. His own belief that the third and last fall was not far distant, in spite of the evidence of the map, gradually gained possession of his companions, and the nerves of all three were keyed to the highest tension of expectancy. The preceding night Mukoki had made himself a paddle to replace the one he had broken, and not a stroke of the three pairs of arms was lost. Early in the morning a young moose allowed them to pass within a hundred yards of him. But no shot was fired, for to obtain the meat would have meant an hour's loss of time.

Two hours after the start the country again began taking on a sudden change. From east and west the wild mountain ridges closed in, and with each mile's progress the stream narrowed and grew swifter, until again it was running between chasm walls that rose black and silent over the adventurers' heads. Darker and gloomier became the break between the mountains. Far above, a thousand feet or more, dense forests of red pine flung their thick shadows over the edge of the chasm, in places almost completely shutting out the light of day. This was not like the other chasm. It was deeper and darker and more sullen. Under its walls the gloom was almost that of night. Its solitude was voiceless; not a bird fluttered or chirped among its rocks; the lowest of whispered words sounded with startling distinctness. Once Rod spoke aloud, and his voice rose and beat itself in the cavernous depths of the walls until it seemed as though he had shouted. Now they ceased paddling, and Mukoki steered. Noiselessly the current swept them on. In the twilight gloom Rod's face shone with singular whiteness. Mukoki and Wabigoon crouched like bronze silhouettes. It was as if some mysterious influence held them in its power, forbidding speech, holding their eyes in staring expectancy straight ahead, filling them with indefinable sensations that made their hearts beat faster and their blood tingle.

Softly, from far ahead, at last there came a murmur. It was like the first gentle whispering of an approaching wind, the soughing of a breath among the pines at the top of the chasm. But a wind among the trees rises, and then dies away, like a chord struck low and gently upon some soft-toned instrument. This whisper that came up the chasm remained. It grew no louder, and sometimes it almost faded away, until the straining ears of those who listened could barely detect it; but after a moment it was there again, as plainly as before. Little by little it became more distinct, until there were no longer intervals when it died away, and at last Wabigoon turned in the bow and faced his companions, and though he spoke no word there was the gleam of a great excitement in his eyes. Rod's heart beat like a drum. He, too, began to understand. That moaning, whispering sound floating up the chasm was not the wind, but the far-away rumble of the third waterfall!

Mukoki's voice broke the tense silence from behind.

"That the fall!"

Wabigoon replied in words scarcely louder than a whisper. There was no joyful shouting now, as there had been at the discovery of the second fall. Even Mukoki's voice was so low that the others could barely hear. Something between these chasm walls seemed to demand silence from them, and as the rumble of the cataract came more and more clearly to their ears they held their breath in voiceless anticipation. A few hundred yards ahead of them was the treasure which men long since dead had discovered more than half a century before; between the black mountain walls that so silently guarded that treasure there seemed to lurk the spirit presence of the three men who had died because of it. Here, somewhere very near, John Ball had been murdered, and Rod almost fancied that along the sandy edge of the chasm stream they might stumble on the footprints of the men whose skeletons they had discovered in the ancient cabin.

Mukoki uttered no sound as he guided the canoe ashore. Still without word, the three picked up their rifles and Wabigoon led the way along the edge of the stream. Soon it dashed a swift racing torrent between the rocks, and Rod and his companions knew that they were close upon the fall. A hundred yards or more and they saw the white mist of it leaping up before their eyes. Wabi began to run, his moccasined feet springing from stone to stone with the caution of a hunter approaching game, and Mukoki and Rod came close behind him.

They paused upon the edge of a great mass of rock with the spray of the plunging cataract rising in their faces. Breathless they gazed down. It was not a large fall. Wabi silently measured it at forty feet. But it added just that much more to the depth and the gloom of the chasm beyond, into which there seemed no way of descent. The rock walls rose sheer and black, with clumps of cedar and stunted pine growing at their feet. Farther on the space between the mountains became wider, and the river reached out on either side, frothing and beating itself into white fury in a chaos of slippery water-worn rocks.

Down there—somewhere—was the golden treasure they had come to seek, unless the map lied! Was it among those rocks, where the water dashed and fumed? Was it hidden in some gloomy cavern of the mountain sides, its trail concealed by the men who discovered it half an age ago? Would they find it, after all—would they find it?

A great gulp of excitement rose in Rod's throat, and he looked at Wabigoon.

The Indian youth had stretched out an arm. His eyes were blazing, his whole attitude was one of tense emotion.

"There's the cabin," he cried, "the cabin built by John Ball and the two Frenchmen! See, over there among those cedars, almost hidden in that black shadow of the mountain! Great Scott, Muky—Rod—can't you see? Can't you see?"

CHAPTER XIV

THE PAPER IN THE OLD TIN BOX

Slowly out of that mysterious gloom there grew a shape before Rod's eyes. At first it was only a shadow, then it might have been a rock, and then the gulp in his throat leaped out in a shout when he saw that Wabigoon's sharp eyes had in truth discovered the old cabin of the map. For what else could it be? What else but the wilderness home of the adventurers whose skeletons they had found, Peter Plante and Henri Langlois, and John Ball, the man whom these two had murdered?

Rod's joyous voice was like the touch of fire to Wabi's enthusiasm and in a moment the oppressive silence of their journey down the chasm was broken by the wild cheers which the young gold seekers sent echoing between the mountains. Grimacing and chuckling in his own curious way, Mukoki was already slipping along the edge of the rock, seeking some break by which he might reach the lower chasm. They were on the point of turning to the ascent of the mountain, along which they would have to go until they found such a break, when the old pathfinder directed the attention of his companions to the white top of a dead cedar stub projecting over the edge of the precipice.

"Go down that, mebby," he suggested, shrugging his shoulders to suggest that the experiment might be a dangerous one.

Rod looked over. The top of the stub was within easy reach, and the whole tree was entirely free of bark or limbs, a fact which in his present excitement did not strike him as especially unusual. Swinging his rifle strap over his shoulders he reached out, caught the slender apex of the stub, and before the others could offer a word of encouragement or warning was sliding down the wall of the rock into the chasm. Wabi was close behind him, and not waiting for Mukoki's descent the two boys hurried toward the cabin. Half-way to it Wabi stopped.

"This isn't fair. We've got to wait for Muky."

They looked back. Mukoki was not following. The old warrior was upon his knees at the base of the dead tree, as though he was searching for something among the rocks at its foot. Then he rose slowly, and rubbed his hands along the stub as high as he could reach. When he saw that Rod and Wabi were observing him he quickly came toward them, and Wabigoon, who was quick to notice any change in him, was confident that he had made a discovery of some kind.

"What have you found, Muky?"

"No so ver' much. Funny tree," grunted the Indian.

"Smooth as a fireman's brass pole," added Rod, seeing no significance in Mukoki's words. "Listen!"

He stopped so suddenly that Wabigoon bumped into him from behind.

"Did you hear that?"

"No."

For a few moments the three huddled close together in watchful silence. Mukoki was behind the boys or they would have seen that his rifle was ready to spring to his shoulder and that his black eyes were snapping with something not aroused by curiosity alone. The cabin was not more than twenty paces away. It was old, so old that Rod wondered how it had withstood the heavy storms of the last winter. A growth of saplings had found root in its rotting roof and the logs of which it was built were in the last stage of decay. There was no window, and where the door had once been there had grown a tree a foot in diameter, almost closing the narrow aperture through which the mysterious inhabitants had passed years before. A dozen paces, five paces from this door, and Mukoki's hand reached out and laid itself gently upon Wabi's shoulder. Rod saw the movement and stopped. A strange look had come into the old Indian's face, an expression in which there was incredulity and astonishment, as if he believed and yet doubted what his eyes beheld. Mutely he pointed to the tree growing before the door, and to the reddish, crumbling rot into which the logs had been turned by the passing of generations.

"Red pine," he said at last. "That cabin more'n' twent' t'ous'nd year old!"

There was an awesome ring in his voice. Rod understood, and clutched Wabi's arm. In an instant he thought of the other old cabin, in which they had found the skeletons. They had repaired that cabin and had passed the winter in it, and they knew that it had been built half a century or more before. But this cabin was beyond repair. To Rod it seemed as though centuries of time instead of decades had been at work on its timbers. Following close after Wabi he thrust his head through the door. Deep gloom shut out their vision. But as they looked, steadily inuring their eyes to the darkness within, the walls of the old cabin took form, and they saw that everywhere was vacancy. There was no ancient table, as in the other cabin they had discovered at the head of the first chasm, there were no signs of the life that had once existed, not even the remnants of a chair or a stool. The cabin was bare.

Foot by foot the two boys went around its walls. Mukoki took but a single glance inside and disappeared. Once alone he snapped down the safety of his rifle. Quickly, as if he feared interruption, he hurried around the old cabin, his eyes close to the earth. When Rod and Wabi returned to the door he was at the edge of the fall, crouching low among the rocks like an animal seeking a trail. Wabi pulled his companion back.

"Look!"

The old warrior rose, suddenly erect, and turned toward them, but the boys were hidden in the gloom. Then he hurried to the dead stub beside the chasm wall. Again he reached far up, rubbing his hand along its surface.

"I'm going to have a look at that tree!" whispered Wabi. "Something is puzzling Are you coming?"

He hurried across the rock-strewn opening, but Rod hung back. He could not understand his companions. For weeks and months they had planned to find this third waterfall. Visions of a great treasure had been constantly before their eyes, and now that they were here, with the gold perhaps under their very feet, both Mukoki and Wabigoon were more interested in a dead stub than in their search for it! His own heart was almost bursting with excitement. The very air which he breathed in the old cabin set his blood leaping with anticipation. Here those earlier adventurers had lived half a century or more ago. In it the life-blood of the murdered John Ball might have ebbed away. In this cabin the men whose skeletons he had found had slept, and planned, and measured their gold. And the gold! It was that and not the stub that interested Roderick Drew! Where was the lost treasure? Surely the old cabin must hold some clue for them, it would at least tell them more than the limbless white corpse of a tree!

From the door he looked back into the dank gloom, straining his eyes to see, and then glanced across the opening. Wabi had reached the stub, and both he and Mukoki were on their knees beside it. Probably they have found the marks of a lynx or a bear, thought Rod. A dozen paces away something else caught his eyes, a fallen red pine, dry and heavy with pitch, and in less than a minute he had gone to it and was back with a torch. Breathlessly he touched the tiny flame of a match to the stick. For a moment the pitch sputtered and hissed, then flared into light, and Rod held the burning wood above his head.

The young gold seeker's first look about him was disappointing. Nothing but the bare walls met his eyes. Then, in the farthest corner, he observed something that in the dancing torch-light was darker than the logs themselves, and he moved toward it. It was a tiny shelf, not more than a foot long, and upon it was a small tin box, black and rust-eaten by the passing of ages. With trembling fingers Rod took it in his hand. It was very light, probably empty. In it he might find the dust of John Ball's last tobacco. Then, suddenly, as he thought of this, he stopped in his search and a muffled exclamation of surprise fell from him. In the glow of the torch he looked at the tin box. It was crumbling with age and he might easily have crushed it in his hand—and yet it was still a tin box! If this box had remained why had not other things? Where were the pans and kettles, the pail and frying-pan, knives, cups and other articles which John Ball and the two Frenchmen must at one time have possessed in this cabin?

He returned to the door. Mukoki and Wabigoon were still at the dead stub. Even the flare of light in the old cabin had not attracted them. Tossing his torch away Rod tore off the top of the tin box. Something fell at his feet, and as he reached for it he saw that it was a little roll of paper, almost as discolored as the rust-eaten box itself. As gently as Mukoki had unrolled the precious birchbark map a few months before he smoothed out the paper. The edges of it broke and crumbled under his fingers, but the inner side of the roll was still quite white. Mukoki and Wabigoon, looking back, saw him suddenly turn toward them with a shrill cry on his lips, and the next instant he was racing in their direction, shouting wildly at every step.

"The gold!" he shrieked. "The gold! Hurrah!"

He was almost sobbing in his excitement when he stopped between them, holding out the bit of paper.

"I found it in the cabin—in a tin box! See, it's John Ball's writing—the writing that was on the old map! I found it—in a tin box—"

Wabi seized the paper. His own breath came more quickly when he saw what was upon it. There were a few lines of writing, dim but still legible, and a number of figures. Across the top of the paper was written,

"Account of John Ball, Henri Langlois, and Peter Plante for month ending June thirtieth, 1859."

Below these lines was the following:

"Plante's work: nuggets, 7 pounds, nine ounces; dust, 1 pound, 3
ounces. Langlois' work: nuggets, 9 pounds, 13 ounces; dust, none.
Ball's work: nuggets, 6 pounds, 4 ounces; dust, 2 pounds, 3 ounces.
Total, 27 pounds.
Plante's share, 6 pounds, 12 ounces.
Langlois' share, 6 pounds, 12 ounces.
Ball's share, 13 pounds, 8 ounces.
Division made."

Softly Wabigoon read the words aloud. When he finished his eyes met Rod's, Mukoki was still crouching at the foot of the stub, staring at the two boys in silence, as if stupefied by what he had just heard.

"This doesn't leave a doubt," said Wabi at last. "We've struck the right place!"

"The gold is somewhere—very near—"

Rod could not master the tremble in his voice. As though hoping to see the yellow treasure heaped in a pile before his eyes he turned to the waterfall, to the gloomy walls of the chasm, and finally extended an arm to where the spring torrent, leaping over the edge of the chasm above, beat itself into frothing rage among the rocks between the two mountains.

"It's there!"

"In the stream?"

"Yes. Where else near this cabin would they have found pure nuggets of gold? Surely not in rock! And gold-dust is always in the sands of streams. It's there—without a doubt!"

Both Indians went with him to the edge of the water.

"The creek widens here until it is very shallow," said Wabi. "I don't believe that it is more than four feet deep out there in the middle. What do you say—" He paused as he saw Mukoki slip back to the dead stub again, then went on, "What do you say to making a trip to the canoe after grub for our dinner, and the pans?"

The first flash of enthusiasm that had filled Wabigoon on reading the paper discovered by Rod was quickly passing away, and the white youth could not but notice the change which came over both Mukoki and his young friend when they stood once more beside the smooth white stub that reached up to the floor of the chasm above. He controlled his own enthusiasm enough to inspect more closely the dead tree which had affected them so strangely. The discovery he made fairly startled him. The surface of the stub was not only smooth and free of limbs, but was polished until it shone with the reflecting luster of a waxed pillar! For a moment he forgot the paper which he held in his hand, forgot the old cabin, and the nearness of gold. In blank wonder he stared at Mukoki, and the old Indian shrugged his shoulders.

"Ver' nice an' smooth!"

"Ver' dam' smooth!" emphasized Wabi, without a suggestion of humor in his voice.

"What does it mean?" asked Rod.

"It means," continued Wabigoon, "that this old stub has for a good many years been used! by something as a sort of stairway in and out of this chasm! Now if it were a bear, there would be claw marks. If it were a lynx, the surface of the stub would be cut into shreds. Any kind of animal would have left his mark behind, and no animal would have put this polish on it!"

"Then what in the world—"

Rod did not finish. Mukoki lifted his shoulders to a level with his chin, and Wabi whistled as he looked straight at him.

"Not a hard guess, eh?"

"You mean—"

"That it's a man! Only the arms and legs of a man going up and down that stub hundreds and thousands of times could have worn it so smooth! Now, can you guess who that man is?"

In a flash the answer shot into Rod's brain. He understood now why this old stub had drawn his companions away from their search for gold, and he felt the flush of excitement go out of his own cheeks, and an involuntary thrill pass up his back.

"The mad hunter!"

Wabi nodded. Mukoki grunted and rubbed his hands.

"Gold in bullet come from here!" said the old pathfinder. "Bad dog man ver' swift on trail. We hurry get canoe—cut down tree!"

"That's more than you've said in the last half-hour, and it's a good idea!" exclaimed Wabi. "Let's get our stuff down here and chop this stub into firewood! When he comes back and finds his ladder gone he'll give a screech or two, I'll wager, and then it will be our chance to do something with him. Here goes!"

He started to climb the stub, and a minute or two later stood safely on the rock above.

"Slippery as a greased pole!" he called down. "Bet you can't make it, Rod!"

But Rod did, after a tremendous effort that left him breathless and gasping by the time Wabi stretched out a helping hand to him. Mukoki came up more easily. Taking only their revolvers with them the three hurried to the birch bark, and in a single load brought their possessions to the rock. By means of ropes the packs and other contents of the canoe, and finally the canoe itself, were lowered into the chasm, and while the others looked on Mukoki seized the ax and chopped down the stub.

"There!" he grunted, as a last blow sent the tree crashing among the rocks. "Too high for heem jump!"

"But a mighty good place for him to shoot from," said Wabi, looking up. "We'd better camp out of range."

"Not until we know what we've struck," cried Rod, unstrapping a pan from one of the packs. "Boys, the first thing to do is to wash out a little of that river-bed!"

He started for the creek, with Wabi close behind him bearing a second pan. Mukoki looked after them and chuckled softly to himself as he began making preparations for dinner. Choosing a point where the current had swept up a small bar of pebbles and sand Wabi and Rod both set to work. The white youth had never before panned gold, but he had been told how it was done, and there now shot through him that strange, thrilling excitement which enthralls the treasure hunter when he believes that at last he has struck pay dirt. Scooping up a quantity of the gravel and sand he filled his pan with water, then moved it, quickly back and forth, every few moments splashing some of the "wash" or muddy water, over the side. Thus, filling and refilling his pan with fresh water, he excitedly went through the process of "washing" everything but solid substance out of it.

With each fresh dip into the stream the water in the pan became clearer, and within fifteen minutes the three or four double handfuls of sand and gravel with which he began work dwindled down to one. Scarcely breathing in his eagerness he watched for the yellow gleam of gold. Once a glitter among the pebbles drew a low cry from him, but when with the point of his knife he found it to be only mica he was glad that Wabi had not heard him. The young Indian was squatting upon the sand, with his pan turned toward a gleam of the sun that shot faintly down into the chasm. Without raising his head he called to Rod.

"Found anything?"

"No. Have you?"

"No—yes—but I don't think it's gold"

"What does it look like?"

"It gleams yellow but is as hard as steel."

"Mica!" said Rod.

Neither of the boys looked up during the conversation. With the point of his hunting-knife Rod still searched in the bottom of his pan, turning over the pebbles and raking the gravelly sand with a painstaking care that would have made a veteran gold seeker laugh. Some minutes had passed when Wabi spoke again.

"I say, Rod, that's a funny-looking thing I found! If it wasn't so hard I'd swear it was gold? Want to see it?"

"It's mica," repeated Rod, as another gleam, of "fool's gold" in his own pan caught his eyes. "The stream is full of it!"

"Never saw mica in chunks before," mumbled Wabi, bending low over his pan.

"Chunks!" cried Rod, straightening as if some one had run a pin into his back. "How big is it?"

"Big as a pea—a big pea!"

The words were no sooner out of the young Indian's mouth than Roderick was upon his feet and running to his companion.

"Mica doesn't come in chunks! Where—"

He bent over Wabi's pan. In the very middle of it lay a suspiciously yellow pebble, worn round and smooth by the water, and when Rod took it in his fingers he gave a low whistle of mock astonishment as he gazed down into Wabigoon's face.

"Wabi, I'm ashamed of you!" he said, trying hard to choke back the quiver in his voice. "Mica doesn't come in round chunks like this. Mica isn't heavy. And this is *both*!"

From the cedars beyond the old cabin came Mukoki's whooping signal that dinner was ready.

CHAPTER XV

THE TREASURE IN THE POOL

For a few moments after Rod's words and Mukoki's signal from the cedars Wabigoon sat as if stunned.

"It isn't—gold," he said, his voice filled with questioning doubt.

"That's just what it is!" declared Rod, his words now rising in the excitement which he was vainly striving to suppress. "It's hard, but see how your knife point has scratched it! It weighs a quarter of an ounce! Are there any more nuggets in there?"

He fell upon his knees beside Wabi, and their two heads were close together, their four eyes eagerly searching the contents of the pan, when Mukoki came up behind them. Rod passed the golden nugget to the old Indian, and rose to his feet.

"That settles it, boys. We've hit the right spot. Let's give three cheers for John Ball and the old map, and go to dinner!"

"I agree to dinner, but cut out the cheers." said Wabi, "or else let's give them under our breath. Notice how hollow our voices sound in this chasm! I believe we could hear a shout half a dozen miles away!"

For their camp Mukoki had chosen a site in the edge of the cedars, and had spread dinner on a big flat rock about which the three now gathered. For inspiration, as Wabi said, the young Indian placed the yellow nugget in the center of the improvised table, and if the enthusiasm with which they hurried through their meal counted for anything there was great merit in the golden centerpiece. Mukoki joined the young gold seekers when they again returned to the chasm stream, and the quest of the yellow treasure was vigorously renewed in trembling and feverish expectancy.

Only those who have lived in this quest and who have pursued that elusive *ignis fatuus* of all nations—the lure of gold—can realize the sensations which stir the blood and heat the brain of the treasure seeker as he dips his pan into the sands of the stream where he believes nature has hidden her wealth. As Roderick Drew, a child of that civilization where the dollar is law as well as might, returned to the exciting work which promised him a fortune he seemed to be in a half dream. About him, everywhere, was gold! For no moment did he doubt it; not for an instant did he fear that there might be no more gold in the sand and gravel from which Wabigoon's nugget had come. Treasure was in the very sandbar under his feet! It was out there among the rocks, where the water beat itself angrily into sputtering froth; it was under the fall, and down in the chasm, everywhere, everywhere about him. In one month John Ball and his companions had gathered twenty-seven pounds of it, a fortune of nearly seven thousand dollars! And they had gathered it here! Eagerly he scooped up a fresh pan of the precious earth. He heard the swish-swish of the water in Wabigoon's and Mukoki's pans. But beyond this there were no sounds made by them.

In these first minutes of treasure seeking no words were spoken. Who would give the first shout of discovery? Five minutes, ten, fifteen of them passed, and Rod found no gold. As he emptied his pan he saw Wabi scooping up fresh dirt. He, too, had failed. Mukoki had waded out waist deep among the rocks. A second and a third pan, and a little chill of disappointment cooled Rod's blood. Perhaps he had chosen an unlucky spot, where the gold had not settled! He moved his position, and noticed that Wabigoon had done the same. A fourth and a fifth pan and the result was the same. Mukoki had waded across the stream, which was shallow below the fall, and was working on the opposite side. A sixth pan, and Rod approached the young Indian. The excitement was gone out of their faces. An hour and a half—and no more gold!

"Guess we haven't hit the right place, after all," said Wabi.

"It must be here," replied Rod. "Where there is one nugget there must be more. Gold is heavy, and settles. Perhaps it's deeper down in the river bed."

Mukoki came across to join them. Out among the rocks he had found a fleck of gold no larger than the head of a pin, and this new sign gave them all fresh enthusiasm. Taking off their boots both Rod and Wabi joined the old pathfinder in midstream. But each succeeding pan added to the depressing conviction that was slowly replacing their hopes. The shadows in the chasm began growing longer and deeper. Far overhead the dense canopies of red pine shut out the last sun-glow of day, and the gathering gloom between the mountains gave warning that in this mysterious world of the ancient cabin the dusk of night was not far away. But not until they could no longer see the gleaming mica in their pans did the three cease work. Wet to the waist, tired, and with sadly-shattered dreams they returned to their camp. For a short time Rod's hopes were at their lowest ebb. Was it possible that there was no more gold, that the three adventurers of long ago had discovered a "pocket" here, and worked it out? The thought had been growing in his head. Now it worried him.

But his depression did not last long. The big fire which Mukoki built and the stimulating aroma of strong coffee revived his natural spirits, and both Wabi and he were soon laughing and planning again as they made their cedar-bough shelter. Supper on the big flat stone—a feast of bear steak, hot-stone biscuits, coffee, and that most delectable of all wilderness luxuries, a potato apiece,—and the two irrepressible young gold hunters were once more scheming and building their air-castles for the following day. Mukoki listened, and attended to the clothes drying before the fire, now and then walking out into the gloom of the chasm to look up to where the white rim of the fall burst over the edge of the great rock above them. All that afternoon Wabi and Rod had forgotten the mad hunter and the strange, smoothly worn tree. Mukoki had not.

In the glow of the camp-fire the two boys read over again the old account of John Ball and the two Frenchmen. The tiny slip of paper, yellow with age, was the connecting link between them and the dim and romantic past, a relic of the grim tragedy which these black and gloomy chasm walls would probably keep for ever a secret.

"Twenty-seven pounds," repeated Rod, as if half to himself. "That was one month's work!"

"Pretty nearly a pound a day!" gasped Wabi. "I tell you, Rod, we haven't hit the right spot—yet!"

"I wonder why John Ball's share was twice that of his companions'? Do you suppose it was because he discovered the gold in the first place?" speculated Rod.

"In all probability it was. That accounts for his murder. The Frenchmen were getting the small end of the deal."

"Eighteen hundred fifty-nine," mused Rod. "That was forty-nine years ago, before the great Civil War. Say—"

He stopped and looked hard at Wabigoon.

"Did it ever strike you that John Ball might not have been murdered?"

Wabi leaned forward with more than usual eagerness.

"I have had a thought—" he began.

"What?"

"That perhaps he was not killed."

"And that after the two Frenchmen died in the knife duel he returned and got the gold," continued Rod.

"No, I had not thought of that," said Wabi. Suddenly he rose to his feet and joined Mukoki out in the gloom of the chasm.

Rod was puzzled. Something in his companion's voice, in his face and words, disturbed him. What had Wabigoon meant?

The young Indian soon rejoined him, but he spoke no more of John Ball.

When the two boys went to their blankets Mukoki still remained awake. For a long time he sat beside the fire, his hands gripping the rifle across his knees, his head slightly bowed in that statue-like posture so characteristic of the Indian. For fully an hour he sat motionless, and in his own way he was deeply absorbed in thought. Soon after their discovery of the first golden bullet Wabigoon had whispered a few words into his ear, unknown to Rod; and to-night out in the gloom of the chasm, he had repeated those same words. They had set Mukoki's mind working. He was thinking now of something that happened long ago, when, in his reasoning, the wilderness was young and he was a youth. In those days his one great treasure was a dog, and one winter he went with this faithful companion far into the hunting regions of the North, a long moon's travel from his village. When he returned, months later, he was alone. From his lonely hunting shack deep in the solitudes his comrade had disappeared, and had never returned. This all happened before Mukoki met the pretty Indian girl who became his wife, and was afterward killed by the wolves, and he missed the dog as he would have missed a human brother. The Indian's love, even for brutes, is some thing that lives, and more than twenty moons later—two years in the life of a man—he returned once again to the old shack, and there he found Wholdaia, the dog! The animal knew him, and bounded about on three legs for joy, and because of the missing leg Mukoki understood why he had not returned to him two years before. Two years is a long time in the life of a dog, and the gray hairs of suffering and age were freely sprinkled in Wholdaia's muzzle and along his spine.

Mukoki was not thinking of Wholdaia without a reason. He was thinking of Wabigoon's words—and the mad hunter. Could not the mad hunter do as Wholdaia had done? Was it possible that the bad-dog man who shot golden bullets and who screamed like a lynx was the man who had lived there many, many years ago, and whom the boys called John Ball? Those were the thoughts that Wabi had set working in his brain. The young Indian had not suggested this to Rod. He had spoken of it to Mukoki only because he knew the old pathfinder might help him to solve the riddle, and so he had started Mukoki upon the trail.

The next morning, while the others were finishing their breakfast, Mukoki equipped himself for a journey.

"Go down chasm," he explained to Rod "Fin' where get out to plain. Shoot meat."

That day the gold hunters were more systematic in their work, beginning close to the fall, one on each side of the stream, and panning their way slowly down the chasm. By noon they had covered two hundred yards, and their only reward was a tiny bit of gold, worth no more than a dollar, which Rod had found in his pan. By the time darkness again compelled them to stop they had prospected a quarter of a mile down stream without discovering other signs of John Ball's treasure. In spite of their failure they were less discouraged than the previous evening, for this failure, in a way, was having a sedative and healthful effect. It convinced them that there was a hard and perhaps long task ahead of them, and that they could not expect to find their treasure winnowed in yellow piles for them.

Early in the evening Mukoki returned laden with caribou meat, and with the news that the first break in the chasm walls was fully five miles below. The adventurers now regretted that they had chopped down the stub, for it was decided that the next work should be in the stream above the fall, which would necessitate a ten-mile tramp, five miles to the break and five miles back. When the journey was begun at dawn the following morning several days' supplies were taken along, and also a stout rope by means of which the gold hunters could lower themselves back into their old camp when their work above was completed. Rod noticed that the rocks in the stream seemed much larger than when he had first seen them, and he mentioned the fact to Wabigoon.

"The floods are going down rapidly," explained the young Indian. "All of the snow is melted from the sides of the mountains, and there are no lakes to feed this chasm stream. Within a week there won't be more than a few inches of water below the fall."

"And that is when we shall find the gold!" declared Rod with his old enthusiasm. "I tell you, we haven't gone deep enough! This gold has been here for centuries and centuries, and it has probably settled several feet below the surface of the river-bed. Ball and the

Frenchmen found twenty-seven pounds in June, when the creek was practically dry. Did you ever read about the discoveries of gold in Alaska and the Yukon?"

"A little, when I was going to school with you."

"Well, the richest finds were nearly always from three to a dozen feet under the surface, and when a prospector found signs in surface panning he knew there was rich dirt below. Well find our gold in this chasm, and near the fall!"

Rod's confidence was the chief thing that kept up the spirits of the treasure seekers during the next few days, for not the first sign of gold was discovered above the fall. Yard by yard the prospectors worked up the chasm until they had washed its sands for more than a mile. And with the passing of each day, as Wabigoon had predicted, the stream became more and more shallow, until they could wade across it without wetting themselves above their knees. At the close of the fourth day the three lowered themselves over the face of the rock into the second chasm. So convinced was Rod in his belief that the gold was hidden deep down under the creek bed that he dug a four-foot hole by torch-light and that night after supper washed out several pans of dirt in the glow of the camp-fire. He still found no signs of gold.

The next day's exertions left no room for doubt. Beyond two or three tiny flecks of gold the three adventurers found nothing of value in the deeper sand and gravel of the stream. That night absolute dejection settled on the camp. Both Rod and Wabigoon made vain efforts to liven up their drooping spirits. Only Mukoki, to whom gold carried but a fleeting and elusive value, was himself, and even his hopefulness was dampened by the gloom of his companions. Rod could see but one explanation of their failure. Somewhere near the cataract John Ball and the Frenchmen had found a rich pocket of gold, and they had worked it out, probably before the fatal tragedy in the old cabin.

"But how about the mad hunter and his golden bullets?" insisted Wabi, in another effort to brighten their prospects. "The bullets weighed an ounce each, and I'll stake my life they came from this chasm. He knows where the gold is, if we don't!"

"Come back soon!" grunted Mukoki. "Watch heem. Fin' gol'!"

"That's what we'll do!" cried the young Indian, jumping suddenly to his feet and toppling Rod backward off the rock upon which he was sitting. "Come, cheer up, Rod! The gold is here, somewhere, and we're going to find it! I'm heartily ashamed of you; you, whom I thought would never get discouraged!"

Rod was laughing when he recovered from the playful mauling which Wabi administered before he could regain his feet.

"That's right, I deserve another licking! We've got all the spring and summer before us, and if we don't find the gold by the time snow flies we'll come back and try it again next year! What do you say?"

"And bring Minnetaki with us!" added Wabi, jumping into the air and kicking his heels together. "How will you like that, Rod?" He nudged his comrade in the ribs, and in another moment both were puffing and laughing in one of their good-natured wrestling bouts, in which the cat-like agility of the young Indian always won for him in the end.

In spite of momentary times like this, when the natural buoyancy and enthusiasm of the young adventurers rose above their discouragement, the week that followed added to their general depression. For miles the chasm was explored and at the end of the week they had found less than an ounce of gold. If their pans had given them no returns at all their disappointment would have been less, for then, as Wabi said, they could have given up the ghost with good grace. But the few precious yellow grains which they found now and then lured them on, as these same grains have lured other hundreds and thousands since the dawn of civilization. Day after day they persisted in their efforts; night after night about their camp-fire they inspired each other with new hope and made new plans. The spring sun grew stronger, the poplar buds burst into tiny leaf and out beyond the walls of the chasm the first promises of summer came in the sweetly scented winds of the south, redolent with the breath of balsam and pine and the thousand growing things of the plains.

But at last the search came to an end. For three days not even a grain of gold had been found. Around the big rock, where they were eating dinner, Rod and his friends came to a final conclusion. The following morning they would break camp, and leaving their canoe behind, for the creek was now too shallow for even birch-bark navigation, they would continue their exploration of the chasm in search of other adventures. The whole summer was ahead of them, and though they had failed in discovering a treasure where John Ball and the Frenchmen had succeeded, they might find one farther on. At least the trip deeper into the unexplored wilderness would be filled with excitement.

Mukoki rose to his feet, leaving Rod and Wabi still discussing their plans. Suddenly he turned toward them, and a startled cry fell from his lips, while with one long arm he pointed beyond the fall into the upper chasm.

"Listen—heem—heem!"

The old warrior's face twitched with excitement, and for a full half minute he stood motionless, his arm still extended, his black eyes staring steadily at Rod and Wabigoon who sat as silent as the rocks about them. Then there came to them from a great distance a quavering, thrilling sound, a sound that filled them again with the old horror of the upper chasm—the cry of the mad hunter.

At that distant cry Wabigoon sprang to his feet, his eyes leaping fire, his bronzed cheeks whitening in an excitement even greater than that of Mukoki.

"Muky, I told you!" he cried. "I told you!" The young Indian's body quivered, his hands were clenched, and when he turned upon Rod the white youth was startled by the look in his face.

"Rod, John Ball is coming back to his gold!"

Hardly had he spoken the words when the tenseness left his body and his hands dropped to his side.

The words shot from him before he could control himself enough to hold them back. In another moment he was sorry. The thought that John Ball and the mad hunter were the same person he had kept to himself, until for reasons of his own he had let Mukoki into his secret. While the idea had taken larger and larger growth in his mind he knew that from every logical point of view the thing was impossible, and that constraint which came of the Indian blood in him held him from discussing it with Rod. But now the words were out. A quick flush replaced the whiteness that had come into his face. In another instant he was leaning eagerly toward Rod, his eyes kindling into fire again. He had not expected the change that he now saw come over the white youth.

"I have been thinking that for a long time," he continued. "Ever since we found the footprints in the sand. There's just one proof that we need, just one, and—"

"Listen!"

Rod fairly hissed the word as he held up a warning hand.

This time the cry of the mad hunter came to them more distinctly. He was approaching through the upper chasm!

The white youth rose to his feet, his eyes steadily fixed upon Wabigoon's. His face was deathly pale.

"John Ball!" he repeated, as if he had just heard what the other had said. "John Ball!" What seemed to him to be the only truth swept upon him like a flood, and for a score of seconds, in every one of which he could hear his heart thumping excitedly, he stood like one stunned. John Ball! John Ball returned to life to find their gold for them, to tell them of the tragedy and mystery of those days long dead and gone! Like powder touched by a spark of fire his imagination leaped at Wabi's thrilling suggestion.

Mukoki set to work.

"Hide!" he exclaimed. "Hide thees—thees—thees!" He pointed about him at all the things in camp.

Both of the boys understood.

"He must see no signs of our presence from the top of the fall!" cried Wabi, gathering an armful of camp utensils. "Hide them back among the cedars!"

Mukoki hurried to the cedar bough shelter and began tearing it down. For five minutes the adventurers worked on the run. Once during that time they heard the madman's wailing cry, and hardly had they finished and concealed themselves in the gloom of the old cabin when it came again, this time from not more than a rifle-shot's distance beyond the cataract. It was not a scream that now fell from the mad hunter's lips, but a low wail and in it there was something that drove the old horror from the three wildly beating hearts and filled them with a measureless, nameless pity. What change had come over the madman? The cry was repeated every few seconds now, each time nearer than before, and in it there was a questioning, appealing note that seemed to end in sobbing despair, a something that gripped at Rod's heart and filled him with a great half-mastering impulse to answer it, to run out and stretch his hands forth in greeting to the strange, wild creature coming down the chasm!

Then, as he looked, something ran out upon the edge of the great rock beside the cataract, and he clutched at his own breast to hold back what he thought must burst forth in words. For he knew—as surely as he knew that Wabi was at his side—that he was looking upon John Ball! For a moment the strange creature crouched where the stub had been, and when he saw that it was gone he stood erect, and a quavering, pitiful cry echoed softly through the chasm. And as he stood there motionless the watchers saw that the mad hunter was an old man, tall and thin, but as straight as a sapling, and that his head and breast were hidden in shaggy beard and hair. In his hands he carried a gun—the gun that had fired the golden bullets—and even at that distance those who were peering from the gloom of the cabin saw that it was a long barreled weapon similar to those they had found in the other old cabin, along with the skeletons of the Frenchmen who had died in the fatal knife duel.

In breathless suspense the three waited, not a muscle of their bodies moving. Again the old man leaned over the edge of the rock, and his voice came to them in a moaning, sobbing appeal, and after a little he stretched out his arms, still crying softly, as if beseeching help from some one below. The spectacle gripped at Rod's soul. A hot film came into his eyes and there was an odd little tremble in his throat. The Indians were looking with dark, staring eyes. To them this was another unusual incident of the wilderness. But to Rod it was the white man's soul crying out to his own. The old man's outstretched arms seemed reaching to him, the sobbing voice, filled with its pathos, its despair, its hopeless loneliness, seemed a supplication for him to come forth, to reach up his own arms, to respond to this lost soul of the solitudes. With a little cry Rod darted between his companions. He threw off his cap and lifted his white face to the startled creature on the rock, and as he advanced step by step, reaching out his hands in friendship, he called softly a name:

"John Ball, John Ball, John Ball!"

In an instant the mad hunter had straightened himself, half turned to flee.

"John Ball! Hello, John Ball—John Ball—"

In his earnestness Rod was almost sobbing the name. He forgot everything now, everything but that lonely figure on the rock, and he drew nearer and nearer, gently calling the name, until the mad hunter dropped on his knees and, crumpled in his long beard and gray lynx skin, looked down upon Rod and sent back a low moaning, answering cry.

"John Ball! John Ball, is that you?"

Rod stopped, with the madman forty feet above him, and something seemed choking back the very breath in him when he saw the strange look that had come into the old man's eyes.

"John Ball—"

The wild eyes above shifted for a moment. They caught a glimpse of two heads thrust from the door of the old cabin, and the madman sprang to his feet. For a breath he stood on the edge of the rock, then with a cry he leaped with the fierce agility of an animal far out into the swirl of the cataract! For an instant he was visible in the downward plunge of the water. Another instant and with a heavy splash he disappeared in the deep pool under the fall!

Wabi and Mukoki had seen the desperate leap and the young Indian was beside the pool before Rod had recovered from his horrified astonishment. For centuries the water of the chasm stream had been tumbling into this pool wearing it deeper and deeper each year, until the water in it was over a man's head. In width it was not more than a dozen feet.

"Watch for him! He'll drown if we don't get him out," shouted Wabi.

Rod leaped to the edge of the pool, with Mukoki between him and Wabigoon. Ready to spring into the cold depths at the first sign of the old man's gray head or struggling arms the three stood with every muscle ready for action. A second, two seconds, five seconds passed, and there was no sign of him. Rod's heart began to beat with drum-like fierceness. Ten seconds! A quarter of a minute! He looked at Wabigoon. The young Indian had thrown off his caribou-skin coat; his eyes, as he turned them for a moment toward Rod, flashed back the white youth's fear.

"I'm going to dive for him!"

In another instant he had plunged head foremost into the pool. Mukoki's coat fell to the ground. He crouched forward until it seemed he must topple from the stone upon which he stood. Another fifteen seconds and Wabigoon's head appeared above the water, and the old warrior gave a shout.

"Me come!"

He shot out and disappeared in a huge splash close to Wabi. Rod stood transfixed, filled with a fear that was growing in him at every breath he drew. He saw the convulsions of the water made by the two Indians, who were groping about below the surface. Wabigoon came up again for breath, then Mukoki. It seemed to him that an age had passed, and he felt no hope. John Ball was dead!

Not for a moment now did he doubt the identity of the mad hunter. The strange, wistful light that had replaced the glare in the old man's eyes when he heard his own name called to him had spoken more than words. It was John Ball! And he was dead! For a third time, a fourth, and a fifth Mukoki and Wabigoon came up for air, and the fifth time they dragged themselves out upon the rocks that edged the pool. Mukoki spoke no word but ran back to the camp and threw a great armful of dry fuel upon the fire. Wabigoon still remained at the edge of the pool, dripping and shivering. His hands were clenched, and Rod could see that they were filled with sand and gravel. Mechanically the Indian opened his fingers and looked at what he had unconsciously brought up from under the fall.

For a moment he stared, then with his gasping breath there came a low, thrilling cry.

He held out his hands to Rod.

Gleaming richly among the pebbles which he held was a nugget of pure gold, a nugget so large that Rod gave a wild yell, and in that one moment forgot that John Ball, the mad hunter, was dead or dying beneath the fall!

CHAPTER XVI

JOHN BALL AND THE MYSTERY OF THE GOLD

Mukoki, hearing Rod's cry, hurried to the pool, but before he reached the spot where the white youth was standing with the yellow nugget in his hand Wabigoon had again plunged beneath the surface. For several minutes he remained in the water, and when he once more crawled out upon the rocks there was something so strange in his face and eyes that for a moment Rod believed he had found the dead body of the madman.

"He isn't—in—the—pool!" he panted. Mukoki shrugged his shoulders and shivered.

"Dead!" he grunted

"He isn't in the pool!"

Wabigoon's black eyes gleamed in uncanny emphasis of his words.

"He isn't in the pool!"

The others understood what he meant. Mukoki's eyes wandered to where the water of the pool gushed between the rocks into the broader channel of the chasm stream. It was not more than knee deep!

"He no go out there!"

"No!"

"Then—where?"

He shrugged his shoulders suggestively again, and pointed into the pool.

"Body slip under rock. He there!"

"Try it!" said Wabigoon tersely.

He hurried to the fire, and Rod went with him to gather more fuel while the young Indian warmed his chilled body. They heard the old pathfinder leap into the water under the fall as they ran.

Ten minutes later Mukoki joined them.

"Gone! Bad-dog man no there!"

He stretched out one of his dripping arms.

"Gol' bullet!" he grunted.

In the palm of his hand lay another yellow nugget, as large as a hazelnut!

"I told you," said Wabi softly, "that John Ball was coming back to his gold. And he has done so! The treasure is in the pool!"

But where was John Ball?

Dead or alive, where could he have disappeared?

Under other conditions the chasm would have rung with the wild rejoicing of the gold seekers. But there was something now that stilled the enthusiasm in them. At last the ancient map had given up its secret, and riches were within their grasp. But no one of the three shouted out his triumph. Somehow it seemed that John Ball had died for them, and the thought clutched at their hearts that if they had not cut down the stub he would still be alive. Indirectly they had brought about the death of the poor creature who for nearly half a century had lived alone with the beasts in these solitudes. And that one glimpse of the old man on the rock, the prayerful entreaty in his wailing voice, the despair which he sobbed forth when he found his tree gone, had livened in them something that was more than sympathy. At this moment the three adventurers would willingly have given up all hopes of gold could sacrifice have brought back that sad, lonely old man who had looked down upon them from the wall of the upper chasm.

"I am sorry we cut down the stub," said Rod.

They were the first words spoken.

"So am I," replied Wabi simply, beginning to strip off his wet clothes. "But—" He stopped, and shrugged his shoulders.

"What?"

"Well, we're taking it for granted that John Ball is dead. If he is dead why isn't he in the pool? By George, I should think that Mukoki's old superstition would be getting the best of him!"

"I believe he is in the pool!" declared Rod.

Wabi turned upon him and repeated the words he had spoken to the old warrior half an hour before.

"Try it!"

After the attempts of the two Indians, who could dive like otter, Rod had no inclination to follow Wabi's invitation. Mukoki, who had hung up a half of his clothes near the fire, was fitting one of the pans to the end of a long pole which he had cut from a sapling, and it was obvious that his intention was to begin at once the dredging of the pool for gold. Rod joined him, and once more the excitement of treasure hunting stirred in his veins. When the pan was on securely Wabi left the fire to join his companions, and the three returned to the pool. With a long sweep of his improvised dredge Mukoki scooped up two quarts or more of sand and gravel and emptied it upon one of the flat rocks, and the two boys pounced upon it eagerly, raking it out with their fingers and wiping the mud and sand from every suspicious looking pebble.

"The quickest way is to wash it!" said Rod, as Mukoki dumped another load upon the rock. "I'll get some water!"

He ran to the camp for the remaining pans and when he turned back he saw Wabi leaping in a grotesque dance about the rock while Mukoki stood on the edge of the pool, his dredge poised over it, silent and grinning.

"What do you think of that?" cried the young Indian as Rod hurried to him. "What do you think of that?"

He held out his hand, and in it there gleamed a third yellow nugget, fully twice as large as the one discovered by Mukoki!

Rod fairly gasped. "The pool must be full of 'em!"

He half-filled his pan with the sand and gravel and ran knee-deep out into the running stream. In his eagerness he splashed over a part of his material with the wash, but he, excused himself by thinking that this was his first pan, and that with the rest he would be more careful. He began to notice now that all of the sand was not washing out, and when he saw that it persisted in lying heavy and thick among the pebbles his heart leaped into his mouth. One more dip, and he held his pan to the light coming through the rift in the chasm. A thousand tiny, glittering particles met his eyes! In the center of the pan there gleamed dully a nugget of pure gold as big as a pea! At last they had struck it rich, so rich that he trembled as he stared down into the pan, and the cry that had welled up in his throat was choked back by the swift, excited beating of his heart. In that moment's glance down into his treasure-laden pan he saw all of his hopes and all of his ambitions achieved. He was rich! In those gleaming particles he saw freedom for his mother and himself. No longer a bitter struggle for existence in the city, no more pinching and striving and sacrifice that they might keep the little home in which his father had died! When he turned toward Wabigoon his face was filled with the ecstasy of those visions. He waded ashore and held his pan under the other's eyes.

"Another nugget!" exclaimed Wabi excitedly.

"Yes. But it isn't the nugget. It's the—" He moved the pan until the thousand little particles glittered and swam before the Indian's eyes. "It's the dust. The sand is full of gold!"

His voice trembled, his face was white. From his crouching posture Wabi looked up at him, and they spoke no more words.

Mukoki looked, and was silent. Then he went back to his dredging. Little by little Rod washed down his pan. Half an hour later he showed it again to Wabigoon. The pebbles were gone. What sand was left was heavy with the gleaming particles, and half buried in it all was the yellow nugget! In Wabi's pan there was no nugget but it was rich with the gleam of fine gold.

Mukoki had dredged a bushel of sand and gravel from the pool, and was upon his knees beside the heap which he had piled on the rock. When Rod went to that rock for his third pan of dirt the old warrior made no sign that he had discovered anything. The early gloom of afternoon was beginning to settle between the chasm walls, and at the end of his fourth pan Rod found that it was becoming so dark that he could no longer distinguish the yellow particles in the sand. With the exception of one nugget he had found only fine gold. With Wabi's dust were three small nuggets.

When they ceased work Mukoki rose from beside the rock, chuckling, grimacing, and holding out his hand. Wabi was the first to see, and his cry of astonishment drew Rod quickly to his side. The hollow of the old warrior's hand was filled with nuggets! He turned them into Wabigoon's hand, and the young Indian turned them into Rod's, and as he felt the weight of the treasure he held Rod could no longer restrain the yell of exultation that had been held in all that afternoon. Jumping high into the air and whooping at every other step he raced to the camp and soon had the small scale which they had brought with them from Wabinosh House. The nuggets they had found that afternoon weighed full seven ounces, and the fine gold, after allowing the deduction of a third for sand, weighed a little more than eleven ounces.

"Eighteen ounces—and a quarter!"

Rod gave the total in a voice tremulous with incredulity.

"Eighteen ounces—at twenty dollars an ounce—three hundred and sixty dollars!" he figured rapidly. "By George—" The prospect seemed too big for him, and he stopped.

"Less than half a day's work," added Wabi. "We're doing better than John Ball and the Frenchmen. It means eighteen thousand dollars a month!"

"And by autumn—" began Rod.

He was interrupted by the inimitable chuckling laugh of Mukoki and found the old warrior's face a map of creases and grimaces.

"In twent' t'ous'nd moon—mak' heem how much?" he questioned.

In all his life Wabigoon had never heard Mukoki joke before, and with a wild whoop of joy he rolled the stoical old pathfinder off the rock on which he was sitting, and Rod joined heartily in Wabi's merriment.

And Mukoki's question proved not to be so much of a joke after all, as the boys were soon to learn. For several days the work went on uninterrupted. The buckskin bags in the balsam shelter grew heavier and heavier. Each succeeding hour added to the visions of the gold seekers. On the fifth day Rod found seventeen nuggets among his fine gold, one of them as large as the end of his thumb. On the seventh came the richest of all their panning, but on the ninth a startling thing happened. Mukoki was compelled to work ceaselessly to keep the two boys supplied with "pay dirt" from the pool. His improvised dredge now brought up only a handful or two of sand and pebbles at a dip. It was on this ninth day that the truth dawned upon them all.

The pool was becoming exhausted of its treasure!

But the discovery brought no great gloom with it. Somewhere near that pool must be the very source of the treasure itself, and the gold hunters were confident of finding it. Besides, they had already accumulated what to them was a considerable fortune, at least two thousand dollars apiece. For three more days the work continued, and then Mukoki's dredge no longer brought up pebbles or sand from the bottom of the pool.

The last pan was washed early in the morning, and as the warm weather had begun to taint the caribou meat Mukoki and Wabigoon left immediately after dinner to secure fresh meat out on the plains, while Rod remained in camp. The strange thick gloom of night which began to gather in the chasm before the sun had disappeared beyond the plains above was already descending upon him when Rod began preparations for supper. He knew that the Indians would not wait until dark before reëntering the break between the mountains, and confident that they would soon appear he began mixing up flour and water for their usual batch of hot-stone biscuits. So intent was he upon his task that he did not see a shadowy form creeping up foot by foot from the rocks. He caught no glimpse of the eyes that glared like smoldering coals from out of the half darkness between him and the fall.

His first knowledge of another presence came in a low, whining cry, a cry that was not much more than a whisper, and he leaped to his feet, every nerve in his body once more tingling with that excitement which had possessed him when he stood under the rock talking to the madman. A dozen yards away he saw a face, a great, white, ghost-like face, staring at him from out of the thickening shadows, and under that face and its tangled veil of beard and hair he saw the crouching form of the mad hunter!

In that moment Roderick Drew thanked God that he was not afraid. Standing full in the glow of the fire he stretched out his arms, as he had once before reached them out to this weird creature, and again, softly, pleadingly, he called the name of John Ball! There came in reply a faint, almost unheard sound from the wild man, a sound that was repeated again and again, and which sent a thrill into the young hunter, for it was wondrously like the name he was calling: "John Ball! John Ball! John Ball!" And as the mad hunter repeated that sound he advanced, foot by foot, as though creeping upon all fours, and Rod saw then that one of his arms was stretched out to him, and that in the extended hand was a fish.

He advanced a step, reaching out his own hands eagerly, and the wild creature stopped, cringing as if fearing a blow.

"John Ball! John Ball!" he repeated. He thought of no other words but those, and advanced bit by bit as he called them gently again and again. Now he was within ten feet of the old man, now eight, presently he was so near that he might have reached him in a single leap. Then he stopped.

The mad hunter laid down his fish. Slowly he retreated, murmuring incoherent sounds in his beard, then sprang to his feet and with a wailing cry sped back toward the pool. Swiftly Rod followed. He saw the form leap from the rocks at its edge, heard a heavy splash, and all was still!

For many minutes Rod stood with the spray of the cataract dashing in his face. This time the madman's plunge into the cold depths at his feet filled him with none of the horror of that first insane leap from the rock above. Somewhere in that pool the old man was seeking refuge! What did it mean? His eyes scanned the thin sheet of water that plunged down from the upper chasm. It was a dozen feet in width and hid the black wall of rock behind it like a thick veil. What was there just behind that falling torrent? Was it possible that in the wall of rock behind the waterfall there was a place where John Ball found concealment?

Rod returned to camp, convinced that he had at last guessed a solution to the mystery. John Ball was behind the cataract! The strange murmurings of the old man who for a few moments had crouched so close to him still rang in his ears, and he was sure that in these half-articulate sounds had been John Ball's own name. If there had been a doubt in his mind before, it was wiped away now. The mad hunter was John Ball, and with that thought burning in his brain Rod stopped beside the fish—the madman's offering of peace—and turned his face once more back toward the black loneliness of the pool.

Unconsciously a sobbing cry of sympathy fell softly from Rod's lips, and he called John Ball's name again, louder and louder, until it echoed far down the gloomy depths of the chasm. There came no response. Then he turned to the fish. John Ball wished them to be friends, and he had brought this offering! In the firelight Rod saw that it was a curious looking, dark-colored fish, covered with small scales that were almost black. It was the size of a large trout, and yet it was not a trout. The head was thick and heavy, like a sucker's, and yet it was not a sucker. He looked at this head more closely, and gave a sudden start when he saw that it had no eyes!

In one great flood the truth swept upon him, the truth of what lay behind the cataract, of where John Ball had gone! For he held in his hands an eyeless creature of another world, a world hidden in the bowels of the earth itself, a proof that beyond the fall was a great cavern filled with the mystery and the sightless things of eternal night, and that in this cavern John Ball found his food and made his home!

CHAPTER XVII

IN A SUBTERRANEAN WORLD

When Mukoki and Wabigoon returned half an hour later the hot-stone biscuits were still unbaked. The fire was only a bed of coals. Beside it sat Rod, the strange fish upon the ground at his feet. Before Mukoki had thrown down the pack of meat which he was carrying he was showing them this fish. Quickly he related what had happened. He added to this some of the things which he had thought while sitting by the fire. The chief of these things were that just behind the cataract was the entrance to a great cavern, and that in this cavern they would not only find John Ball, but also the rich storehouse of that treasure of which they, had discovered a part in the pool.

And as the night lengthened there was little talk about the gold and much about John Ball. Again and again Rod described the madman's visit, the trembling, pleading voice, the offering of the fish, the eager glow that had come into the wild eyes when he talked to him and called him by name. Even Mukoki's stoic heart was struck by the deep pathos of it all. The mad hunter no longer carried his gun. He no longer sought their lives. In his crazed brain something new and wonderful was at work, something that drew him to them, with the half-fear of an animal, and yet with growing trust. He was pleading for their companionship, their friendship, and deep down in his heart Rod felt that the spark of sanity was not completely gone from John Ball.

When the three adventurers retired to their blankets in the cedar shelter it was not the thought of gold that quickened their blood in anticipation of the morning. The passing of an age would not dull the luster of what they had come to seek. It would wait for them. The greatest of all things—the sympathy of man for man—had stilled that other passion in them. John Ball's salvation, and not more gold, was the day's work ahead of them now.

With the dawn they were up, and by the time it was light enough to see they were ready for the exploration of whatever was hidden behind the fall. In a rubber blanket Wabigoon wrapped a rifle and half a dozen pine torches. Mukoki carried a quantity of cooked meat. Standing on the edge of the pool Rod pointed into the falling torrent.

"He dived straight under," he said. "The opening to the cavern is directly behind the shoot of falling water."

Wabi placed his hat and coat upon a rock.

"I'll try it first. Wait until I come back," he said.

Without another word he plunged into the pool. Minute after minute passed, and he did not reappear. Rod was conscious of a nervous chill creeping into his blood. But Mukoki was chuckling confidently.

"Found heem!" he replied in response to the white youth's inquiring look.

As he spoke Wabigoon came up out of the pool like a great fish. Rod helped him upon the rocks.

"We're two bright ones, we are, Muky!" he exclaimed, as soon as he gained his breath. "Just behind the fall I ran up against the wall of rock we found when we were hunting for John Ball, stood on my feet, and—" he swung his arms suggestively—"there I was, head and shoulders out of water, looking into a hole as big as a house!"

"Dive easy!" warned the old pathfinder, turning to Rod. "Bump head on rock—swush!"

"We won't have to dive," continued Wabi. "The water directly under the fall of the stream isn't more than four feet deep. If we wade into it from over there we can make it easy."

Taking his waterproof bundle the young Indian slipped into the pool close up against the wall of rock that formed the foundation of the upper chasm and plunged straight into the tumbling cataract. Mukoki followed close behind and preparing himself with a long breath Rod hurried into this new experience. For a moment he was conscious of a smothering weight upon him and a thunderous roaring in his ears, and he was borne irresistibly down. There was still air in his lungs when he found himself safely through the deluge so he knew that its passage had taken him only a brief but thrilling instant. For a time he could see nothing. Then he made out a dark form drawing itself up out of the water. Beyond that there lay a chaos of midnight blackness, and he knew that his eyes were staring into the depths of a great cavern!

Gripping the edge of the rock ledge he dragged himself up as both Wabigoon and Mukoki had done, and found his feet upon a soft floor of sand. Suddenly he felt a hand clutch his arm. A half-shout, rising faintly above the wash of the cataract, sounded in his ear.

"Look!"

He wiped the water from his eyes and gazed ahead of him. For a moment he saw nothing. Then, so faintly that at first it appeared no larger than a star, he caught the faint glimmer of a light. As he looked it became more and more distinct, and to his astonishment he saw that it was slowly rising, like a huge will-o'-the-wisp that had suddenly risen from the floor of the cavern to float off into the utter blackness of space above. And even as he stared, gripping Wabi's arm in his excitement, the strange light began to descend, and quickly disappeared!

The two boys saw Mukoki slip off into the gloom, and without questioning his motive they followed close behind. As they progressed the sound of the fall came more and more faintly to their ears. A blackness deeper than the gloom of the darkest night environed them, and the three now held to one another's arms. Rod understood why his companions lighted no torches. Somewhere ahead of them was another light, carried by the mad hunter. His blood thrilled with excitement. Where would John Ball lead them?

Suddenly he became conscious that they were no longer walking on a level floor of sand but that they were ascending, as the light had done. Mukoki stopped and for a full minute they stood and listened. The tumult of the fall came to them in a far, subdued murmur. Beyond that there was not the breath of a sound in the strange world of gloom about them. They were about to start on again when something held them, a whispering, sobbing echo, and Rod's heart seemed to stop its beating. It died away slowly, and a weird stillness fell after it. Then came a low moaning cry, a cry that was human in its agony, and yet which had in it something so near the savage that even Wabigoon found himself trembling as he strained in futile effort to pierce the impenetrable gloom ahead. Before the cry had lost itself in the distances of the cavern Mukoki was leading them on again.

Step by step they followed in the path taken by the strange light. Rod knew that they were climbing a hill of sand, and that just beyond it they would see the light again, but he was not prepared for the startling suddenness with which the next change came. As if a black curtain had dropped from before their eyes the three adventurers beheld a scene that halted them in their tracks. A hundred paces away a huge pitch-pine torch a yard in length was burning in the sand, and crouching in the red glow of this, his arms stretched out as if in the supplication of a strange prayer, was John Ball! Just beyond him was the gleam of water, inky-black in the weird flickerings of the torch, and toward this John Ball reached out in his grief. His voice came up softly to the three watchers now, so low that even in the vast silence of the cavern it could barely be heard. To Roderick Drew it was as if the strange creature below him was sobbing like a heart-broken child, and he whispered in Wabigoon's ear. Then, foot by foot, so gently that his moccasined feet made no sound, he approached the madman.

Half-way to him he paused.

"Hello, John Ball!" he called softly.

The faint light of the torch was falling upon him, and he advanced another step. The murmuring of the wild man ceased, but he made no movement. He still knelt in his rigid posture, his arms stretched toward the black chaos beyond him. Rod came very close to him before he spoke again.

"Is that you, John Ball?"

Slowly the kneeling figure turned, and once more Rod saw in those wild eyes, gleaming brightly now in the torch-light, the softer, thrilling glow of recognition and returning reason. He reached out his own arms and advanced boldly, calling John Ball's name, and the madman made no retreat but crouched lower in the sand, strange, soft sounds again falling from his lips. Rod had come within half a dozen feet of him when he sprang up with the quickness of a cat, and with a wailing cry plunged waist deep into the water. With his arms stretched entreatingly into the mysterious world beyond the torch-light he turned his face to the white youth, and Rod knew that he was trying as best he could to tell him something.

"What is it, John Ball?"

He went to the edge of the black water and waded out until it rose to his knees, his eyes staring into the blackness.

"What is it?"

He, too, pointed with one arm, and the madman gave an excited gesture. Then he placed his hands funnel-shaped to his mouth, as Rod had often seen Wabi and Mukoki do when calling moose, and there burst from him a far-reaching cry, and Rod's heart gave a sudden bound as he listened, for the cry was that of a woman's name!

"Dol—o—res-s-s-s—Dol—o—res-s-s-s—"

The cry died away in distant murmuring echoes, and with an answering cry Rod shouted forth the name which he fancied John Ball had spoken.

"Dolores! Dolores! Dolores!"

There came a sudden leaping plunge, and John Ball was at his feet, clasping him about the knees, and sobbing again and again that name—Dolores. Rod put his arms about the old man's shoulders, and the gray, shaggy head fell against him. The sobbing voice grew lower, the weight of the head greater, and after a little Rod called loudly for Mukoki and Wabigoon, for there was no longer movement or sound from the form at his feet, and he knew that something had happened to John Ball. The two Indians were quickly at his side, and together they carried the unconscious form of Ball within the circle of torch-light. The old man's eyes were closed, his claw-like fingers were clenched fiercely upon his breast, and not until Mukoki placed a hand over his heart did the three know that he was still breathing.

"Now is our time to get him to camp," said Wabi. "Lead the way with the torch, Rod!"

There was not much weight to John Ball, and the two Indians carried him easily. At the fall the rubber blanket was wound about his head and the adventurers plunged under the cataract with their burden. It was an hour after that before the old man opened his eyes again. Rod was close beside him and for a full minute the mad hunter gazed up into his face, then once more he sank off into that strange unconsciousness which had overcome him in the cavern. Rod rose white-faced and turned to Mukoki and Wabigoon.

"I'm afraid—he's dying," he said.

The Indians made no answer. For several minutes the three sat silently about John Ball watching for signs of returning consciousness. At last Mukoki roused himself to take a pot of soup from the fire. The movement seemed to stir John Ball into life, and Rod was at his side again, holding a cup of water to his lips. After a little he helped the old man to sit up, and a spoonful at a time the warm soup was fed to him.

Through the whole of that day he returned to consciousness only for brief intervals, lapsing back into a death-like sleep after each awakening. During one of these periods of unconsciousness Wabi cut short the tangled beard and hair, and for the first time they saw in all its emaciation the thin, ghastly face of the man who, half a century before, had drawn the map that led them to the gold. There was little change in his condition during the night that followed, except that now and then he muttered incoherently, and at these times Rod always caught in his ravings the name that he had heard in the cavern. The next day there was no change. And there was still none on the third. Even Mukoki, who had tried every expedient of wilderness craft in nursing, gave up in despair. So far as they could see John Ball had no fever. Yet three-quarters of the time he lay as if dead. Nothing but soup could be forced between his lips.

On the second day Wabi revisited the subterranean world beyond the cataract. When he came back he had discovered the secret of the treasure in the pool. The gold came from the cavern. The soft sand through which they had followed the strange light was rich in dust and nuggets. During the floods of spring water came into the cavern from somewhere, and flowing for a brief space out through the mouth of the cave brought with it the precious burden of treasure-laden sand which was dumped into the pool. The constant wash of the cataract had caused most of the sand to overflow into the running stream, but the heavier gold-dust and nuggets remained in the trap into which they had fallen.

But the joy that came of this discovery was subdued by thoughts of John Ball. The gold meant everything to Rod, the realization of his hopes and ambitions; and he knew that it meant everything to his mother, and to all those who belonged to Mukoki and Wabigoon. But the gold could wait. They had already accumulated a small fortune, and they could return for the rest a little later. At present they must do something for John Ball, the man to whom they were indebted for all that they had found, and to whom the treasure really belonged. On the third day Rod laid his plans before Wabi and Mukoki.

"We must take John Ball back to the Post as quickly as we can," he said. "It is our only chance of saving him. If we start now, while the water in the creek is deep enough to float our canoe, we can make Wabinosh House in ten or fifteen days."

"It will be impossible to paddle against the swift current," said Wabi.

"That is true. But we can put John Ball into the canoe and tow him up-stream. It will be a long wade and hard work, but—"

He looked at Wabi in silence, then added,

"Do we want John Ball to live, or do we want him to die?"

"If I thought he would live I would wade a thousand miles to save him," rejoined the young Indian. "It means little to us but work. We know where the rest of the gold is and can return to it within a few weeks."

If there had been a doubt in the boys' minds as to the right course to pursue John Ball settled it himself that very afternoon. He awakened from an unusually long stupor. His eyes were burning with a new light, and as Rod bent over him he whispered softly, but distinctly,

"Dolores—Dolores—Where is Dolores?"

"Who is Dolores, John Ball?" whispered the white youth, his heart thumping wildly. "Who is Dolores?"

Ball drew up one of his emaciated hands and clasped it to his head, and a sobbing moan fell from his lips. Then, after a moment, he repeated, as though to himself,

"Dolores—Dolores—Who is Dolores?"

The Indians had come near, and heard. But John Ball said no more. He swallowed a few spoonfuls of soup and fell again into his death-like trance.

"Who is Dolores?" repeated Wabigoon, his face whitening as he looked at Rod. "Is there somebody else in the cavern?"

"He is talking of some one whom he probably knew forty or fifty years ago," replied Rod. But his own face was white. He stared hard at Wabigoon, and a strange look came into Mukoki's face.

"Dolores," he mused, without taking his eyes from Wabi. "It's a woman's name, or a girl's name. We must save John Ball! We must start for Wabinosh House—now!"

"While he's unconscious we can tie the rope about him and hoist him into the upper chasm," quickly added Wabigoon. "Muky, get to work. We move this minute!"

It was still two hours before dusk, and now that they had determined on returning to Wabinosh House the adventurers lost no time in getting under way. Wabi climbed the rope that was suspended from the upper chasm, and that part of their equipment which it was necessary to take back with them was hoisted up by him. Mukoki sheltered the rest in the old cabin. John Ball was drawn up last. For an hour after that, until the gray shadows of night began settling about them, the three waded up the shallow stream, pulling the canoe and its unconscious burden after them. That night the madman was not left unwatched for a minute. Mukoki sat beside him until eleven o'clock. Then Wabi took his turn. A little after midnight Rod was aroused by being violently pulled from his bed of balsam boughs.

"For the love of Heaven, get up!" whispered the young Indian. "He's talking, Rod! He's talking about Dolores, and about some kind of a great beast that's bigger than anything that ever lived up here! Listen!"

The madman was moaning softly.

"I've killed it, Dolores—I've killed it—killed it! Where is Dolores? Where—is—" There came a deep sigh, and John Ball was quiet.

"Killed what?" panted Rod, his heart thumping until it choked him.

"The beast—whatever it was," whispered Wabi. "Rod, something terrible happened in that cavern! We don't know the whole story. The Frenchmen who killed themselves for possession of the birch-bark map played only a small part in it. The greater part was played by John Ball and Dolores!"

For a long time the two listened, but the old man made no sound or movement.

"Better go back to bed," said Wabi. "I thought if he was going to keep it up you would like to hear. I'll call you at two."

But Rod could not sleep. For a long time he lay awake thinking of John Ball and his, strange ravings. Who was Dolores? What terrible tragedy had that black world under the mountains some time beheld? Despite his better reason an indefinable sensation of uneasiness possessed him as the madman's sobbing out of the woman's name recurred to him. He spoke nothing of this to Wabi when he relieved him, and he said nothing of it during the days that followed. They were days of unending toil, of fierce effort to beat out death in the race to Wabinosh House.

For it seemed that the end of time was very near for John Ball. On the fourth day his thin cheeks showed signs of fever, and on the fifth he was tossing in delirium. The race now continued by night as well as by day, only an hour or two of rest being snatched at a time. During these days John Ball babbled ceaselessly of Dolores, and great beasts, and the endless cavern; and now the beasts began taking the form of strange people whose eyes gleamed from out of masses of fur, and who had hands, and flung spears. On the eighth day the madman sank back into his old lethargy. On the fourth day after that the three adventurers, worn and exhausted, reached the shore of Lake Nipigon. Thirty miles across the lake was Wabinosh House, and it was decided that Mukoki and Rod should leave for assistance, while Wabigoon remained with John Ball. The two rolled themselves in their blankets immediately after supper, and after three hours' sleep were awakened by the young Indian. All that night they paddled with only occasional moments of rest. The sun was just rising over the forests when they grounded their canoe close to the Post. As Rod sprang ashore he saw a figure walk slowly out from the edge of the forest an eighth of a mile away. Even at that distance he recognized Minnetaki! He looked at the sharp-eyed Mukoki. He, too, had seen and recognized the girl.

"Muky, I'm going along in the edge of the woods and give her a surprise," said Rod courageously. "Will you wait here?"

Mukoki grinned a nodding assent, and the youth darted into the edge of the forest. He was breathless when he came up a hundred yards behind the girl, screened from view by the trees. Softly he whistled. It was a signal that Minnetaki had taught him on his first trip into the North, and he knew of only two who used it in all that Northland, and those two were the Indian maiden and himself. The girl turned as she heard the trilling note, and Rod drew himself farther back. He whistled again, more loudly than before, and Minnetaki came hesitatingly toward the forest's edge, and when he whistled a third time there came a timid response from her, as if she recognized and yet doubted the notes that floated to her from the shadows of the balsams.

Again Rod whistled, laughing as he drew a little farther back, and again Minnetaki answered, peering in among the trees. He saw the wondering, half-expectant glow in her eyes, and suddenly crying out her name he sprang from his concealment. With a little cry of joy and with hands outstretched Minnetaki ran to meet him.

CHAPTER XVIII

JOHN BALL'S STORY

That same morning two big canoes set out across Lake Nipigon for Wabigoon and John Ball. Mukoki returned with the canoes, but Rod remained at the Post, and not a moment's rest did he have during the whole of that day from the eager questions of those whom he had so completely surprised by his unexpected return. Few stories could have been more thrilling than his, though he told it in the simplest manner possible. Rod's appearance more than his words was evidence of the trials he and his companions had passed through. His face was emaciated to startling thinness by desperate exertion and lack of sleep, and both his face and his hands were covered with scratches and bruises. Not until late in the afternoon did he go to bed, and it was noon the following day when he awoke from his heavy slumber.

The canoes had returned, and John Ball was in the doctor's care. At dinner Rod and Wabi were made to go over their adventures again, and even Mukoki, who had joined them in this reunion, was not allowed to escape the endless questioning of Minnetaki, the factor's wife, and Rod's mother. Rod was seated at the table between Mrs. Drew and Minnetaki. Several times during the conversation he felt the young girl's hand touch his arm. Once, when the factor spoke about their return to the gold in the cavern, this mysterious signaling of Minnetaki's took the form of a pinch that made him squirm. Not until after dinner, and the two were alone, did he begin to comprehend.

"I'm ashamed of you, Roderick Drew!" said the girl, standing before him in mock displeasure. "You and Wabi were the stupidest things I ever saw at dinner! Have you all forgotten your promise to me?—your promise that I should go with you on your next trip? I wanted you to speak about it right there at dinner!"

"But I—I—couldn't!" stammered Rod awkwardly.

"But I'm going!" said Minnetaki decisively. "I'm going with you boys on this next trip— if I have to run away! It's not fair for Wabi and Mukoki and you to leave me alone all of the time. And, besides, I've been making all the arrangements while you were gone. I've won over mamma and your mother, and Maballa, mamma's Indian woman, will go with me. There's just one who says—'No!'" And Minnetaki clasped her hands pathetically.

"And that's papa," completed Rod, laughing.

"Yes."

"Well, if he is the only one against us we stand a good chance of winning."

"I'm going to have mamma and Wabigoon get him by themselves to-night," said the girl. "Papa will do anything on earth for her, and he thinks Wabi is the best boy on earth. Mamma says she will lock the door and won't let him out until he has given his promise. Oh, what a glorious time we'll have!"

"Perhaps he would go with us," suggested Rod.

"No, he couldn't leave the Post. If he went Wabi would have to stay."

Rod was counting on his fingers.

"That means six in our next expedition,—Wabi, Mukoki, John Ball and myself, and you and Maballa. Why, it'll be a regular picnic party!"

Minnetaki's eyes were brimming with fun.

"Do you know," she said, "that Maballa thinks Mukoki is just about the nicest Indian that ever lived? Oh, I'd be so glad if—if—"

She puckered her mouth into a round, red O, and left Rod to guess the rest. It was not difficult for him to understand.

"So would I," he cried. Then he added,

"Muky is the best fellow on earth."

"And Maballa is just as good," said the girl loyally.

The boy held out his hand.

"Let's shake on that, Minnetaki! I'll handle Mukoki, you take care of Maballa. What a picnic this next trip will be!"

"And there'll be lots and lots of adventures, won't there?" asked the girl a little anxiously.

"Plenty of them." Rod became immediately serious. "This will be the most important of all our trips, Minnetaki, that is, if John Ball lives. I haven't told the others, but I believe that great cavern holds something for us besides gold!"

The smile left the girl's face. Her eyes were soft and eager.

"You believe that—Dolores—"

"I don't know what to believe. But—we'll find something there!"

For an hour Rod and Minnetaki talked of John Ball and of the strange things he said in his delirium. Then the girl rejoined Mrs. Drew and the princess mother, while Rod went in search of Mukoki and Wabigoon. That night the big event happened. George Newsome, the factor, gave a reluctant consent which meant that Wabi's sister and Maballa would accompany the adventurers on their next journey into the untraveled solitudes of Hudson Bay.

For a week John Ball hovered between life and death. After that his improvement was slow but sure, and each day added strength to his emaciated body and a new light to his eyes. At the end of the second week there was no question but that he was slowly returning to sanity. Gradually he came to know those who sat beside his bed, and whenever Rod visited him he insisted on holding the youth's hand. At first the sight of Minnetaki or her mother, or of Mrs. Drew, had a startling effect on him and in their presence he would moan ceaselessly the name Rod first heard in the cavern. A little at a time the language of those about him came back to the old man, and bit by bit those who waited and listened and watched learned the story of John Ball. Midsummer came before he could gather the scattered threads of his life in his memory, and even then there were breaks in this story which seemed but trivial things to John Ball, but which to the others meant the passing of forgotten years.

In fact, years played but a small part in the strange story that fell from the old man's lips. "In time," said the Post physician, "he will remember everything. Now only the most important happenings in his life have returned to him."

John Ball could not remember the date when, as a young boy, he left York Factory, on Hudson Bay, to come a thousand miles down to civilization in company with the two Frenchmen who killed themselves in the old cabin. But the slip of paper which Rod had discovered filled that gap. He was the son of the factor at York Factory, and was to spend a year at school in Montreal. On their trip down it was the boy who found gold in the chasm. John Ball could remember none of the details. He only knew that they remained to gather the treasure, and that he, as its discoverer and the son of one of the lords of the Hudson Bay Company, was to receive twice the share of the others, and that in the autumn they were to return to York Factory instead of going on to Montreal. He remembered indistinctly a quarrel over the gold, and after that of writing some sort of agreement, and then, early one morning, he awoke to find the two Frenchmen standing over him, and after that, for a long time, everything seemed to pass as in a dream.

When he awoke into life he was no longer in the chasm, but among a strange people who were so small that they reached barely to his shoulders, and who dressed in fur, and carried spears, and though the sick man said no more about these people those who listened to him knew that he had wandered far north among the Eskimos. They treated him kindly, and he lived among them for a long time, hunting and fishing with them, and sleeping in houses built of ice and snow.

The next that John Ball remembered was of white people. In some way he returned to York Factory, and he knew that when this happened many years had passed, for his father and mother were dead, and there were strangers at the Post. At this time John Ball must have returned fully to his reason again. He remembered, faintly, leading several unsuccessful expeditions in search of the gold which he and the Frenchmen had discovered, and that once he went to a great city, which must have been Montreal, and that he stayed there a long time doing something for the Hudson Bay Company, and met a girl whom he married. When he spoke of the girl John Ball's eyes would glow feverishly and her name would fall from him in a moaning sob. For as yet returning reason had not placed the hand of age upon him. It was as if he was awakening from a deep sleep, and Dolores, his young wife, had been with him but a few hours before.

There came another break in John Ball's life after this. He could not remember how, long they lived in Montreal, but he knew that after a time he returned with his wife into the far North, and that they were very happy, and one summer set off in a canoe to search for the lost chasm together. They found it. How or when he could not remember. After this John Ball's story was filled with wild visions of a great black world where there was neither sun nor moon nor stars, and they found gold and dug it by the light of fires. And one day the woman went a little way back in this world and never came back.

It was then that the old madness returned. In his search for his lost wife John Ball never found the end of the great cavern. He saw strange people, he fought great beasts in this black world that were larger than the biggest moose in the forests, and he told of rushing torrents and thundering cataracts in the bowels of the earth. Even in his returning sanity the old man told these things as true.

George Newsome, the factor, lost no time in writing to the Company at Montreal, inquiring about John Ball, and a month later he received word that a man by that name had worked as an inspector of raw furs during the years 1877 and 1878. He had left Montreal for the North thirty years before. In all probability he soon after went in search of the lost gold, and for more than a quarter of a century had lived as a wild man in the solitudes.

It was at this time in the convalescence of the doctor's patient that Roderick's mother made a suggestion which took the Post by storm. It was that the factor and his family accompany her and Rod back to civilization for a few weeks' visit. To the astonishment of all, and especially to Minnetaki and the princess mother, the factor fell in heartily with the scheme, with the stipulation that the Drews return with them early in the autumn. An agent from the head office of the Company had come up for a month's fishing and he cheerfully expressed his willingness to take charge of affairs at the Post during their absence.

The happiness of Rod and Wabi was complete when Mukoki was compelled to give his promise to go with them. For several days the old warrior withstood their combined assaults, but at last he surrendered when Minnetaki put her arms around his neck and nestled her soft cheek against his leathery face, with the avowal that she would not move a step unless he went with her.

So it happened, one beautiful summer morning, that three big canoes put out into the lake from Wabinosh House and headed into the South, and only Mukoki, of all the seven who were going down into civilization, felt something that was not joy as the forests slipped behind them. For Mukoki was to get a glimpse of a new world, a world far from the land of his fathers, and the loyal heart inside his caribou-skin coat quickened its pulse a little as he thought of the wonderful journey.

Thus began the journey to civilization.

THE END

Made in the USA
Monee, IL
13 August 2022

11560435R00066